Labor Day

ALSO BY JOYCE MAYNARD

Fiction

Baby Love

To Die For

Where Love Goes

The Usual Rules

The Cloud Chamber

Nonfiction

Looking Back

Domestic Affairs

At Home in the World

Internal Combustion

Labor Day

Joyce Maynard

An Imprint of HarperCollins*Publishers*

LABOR DAY. Copyright © 2009 by Joyce Maynard. All rights reserved. Printed in the United States of America. No part of this book may be used or reproduced in any manner whatsoever without written permission except in the case of brief quotations embodied in critical articles and reviews. For information address HarperCollins Publishers, 10 East 53rd Street, New York, NY 10022.

HarperCollins books may be purchased for educational, business, or sales promotional use. For information please write: Special Markets Department, HarperCollins Publishers, 10 East 53rd Street, New York, NY 10022.

FIRST HARPERLUXE EDITION

HarperLuxe™ is a trademark of HarperCollins Publishers

Library of Congress Cataloging-in-Publication Data is available upon request.

ISBN: 978-0-06-189392-6

09 10 11 12 13 ID/RRD 10 9 8 7 6 5 4 3 2

For my sons, Charlie and Wilson Bethel, who taught
me about the hearts of thirteen-year-old boys
by their own loving and endlessly lovable example

Labor Day

Chapter 1

It was just the two of us, my mother and me, after my father left. He said I should count the new baby he had with his new wife, Marjorie, as part of my family too, plus Richard, Marjorie's son, who was six months younger than me though he was good at all the sports I messed up in. But our family was my mother, Adele, and me, period. I would have counted the hamster, Joe, before including that baby, Chloe.

Saturday nights when my father picked me up to take us all out to dinner at Friendly's, he was always wanting me to sit next to her in the backseat. Then he'd pull a pack of baseball cards out of his pocket and lay them on the table in the booth, to split between Richard and me. I always gave mine to Richard. Why not? Baseball was a sore spot for me. When the phys ed teacher said, OK, Henry, you play with the blues, all the other guys on the blue team would groan.

For the most part, my mother never mentioned my father, or the woman he was married to now, or her son, or the baby, but once by mistake, when I left a picture out on the table that he'd given me, of the five of us—the year before, when I went with them to Disney—she had studied it for at least a minute. Stood there in the kitchen, holding the picture in her small, pale hand, her long graceful neck tilted a little to one side as if the image she was looking at contained some great and troubling mystery, though really it was just the five of us, scrunched together in the teacup ride.

I would think your father would be worried about the way that baby's one eye doesn't match with the other, she said. It might be nothing more than a developmental delay, not retardation, but you'd think they'd want to have that child tested. Does she seem slow to you, Henry?

Maybe a little.

I knew it, my mother said. That baby doesn't look anything like you either.

I knew my part, all right. I understood who my real family was. Her.

It was unusual for my mother and me to go out the way we did that day. My mother didn't go places, generally. But I needed pants for school.

OK, she said. Pricemart, then. Like my growing a half inch that summer was something I'd done just to give her a hard time. Not that she wasn't having one already.

The car had turned over the first time she turned the key in the ignition, which was surprising, considering a month might have gone by since the last time we'd gone anywhere in it. She drove slowly, as usual, as if dense fog covered the road, or ice, but it was summer—the last days before school started, the Thursday before Labor Day weekend—and the sun was shining.

It had been a long summer. Back when school first got out, I had hoped maybe we'd go to the ocean over the long expanse of vacation ahead—just for the day— but my mother said the traffic was terrible on the highway and I'd probably get sunburned, since I had his coloring, meaning my father.

All that June after school let out, and all that July, and now just having ended August, I kept wishing something different would happen, but it never did. Not just my father coming to take me to Friendly's and now and then bowling with Richard and Marjorie, and the baby, or the trip he took us on to the White Mountains to a basket-making factory, and a place Marjorie wanted to stop, where they made candles that smelled like cranberries or lemon or gingerbread.

Other than that, I'd watched a lot of television that summer. My mother had taught me how to play solitaire, and when that got old, I tackled places in our house that nobody had cleaned in a long time, which was how I'd earned the dollar fifty that was burning a hole in my pocket, for another puzzle book. These days even a kid as weird as I was would do his playing on a Game Boy or a PlayStation, but back then only certain families had Nintendo; we weren't one of them.

I thought about girls all the time at this point, but there was nothing going on in my life where they were concerned besides thoughts.

I had just turned thirteen. I wanted to know about everything to do with women and their bodies, and what people did when they got together—people of the opposite sex—and what I needed to do so I could get a girlfriend sometime before I turned forty years old. I had many questions about sex, but it was clear my mother was not the person to discuss this with, though she herself brought it up on occasion. In the car, on the way to the store, for instance. Your body is changing, I guess, she said, gripping the wheel.

No comment.

My mother stared straight ahead, as if she was Luke Skywalker, manning the controls of the X-wing jet. Headed to some other galaxy. The mall.

When we got to the store, my mother had gone with me to the boys' section and we'd picked out the pants. Also a pack of underwear.

I guess you'll need shoes, too, she said, in that tone of voice she always had when we went places now, like this whole thing was a bad movie but since we'd bought our tickets we had to stay till the end.

My old ones are still OK, I said. What I was thinking was, if I got shoes on this trip too, it might be a long time before we came here again, where, if I held off on the shoes, we'd have to come back. Once school started I'd need notebooks and pencils, and a protractor, and a calculator. Later, when I brought up the shoes, and she said, Why didn't you tell me when we were at the store last time?, I could point out the rest of the items on my list, and she'd give in.

We finished with the clothes part. I'd put the things I picked out in our cart and headed over to the section where they sold the magazines and paperbacks.

I started flipping through an issue of *Mad,* though what I really wanted was to look at the *Playboy*s. They sealed those up in a plastic wrapper.

Now I could see my mother across the rows of merchandise, wheeling our cart through the aisles. Slowly, like a leaf in a slow-moving creek, just drifting. No telling what she might put in the cart, though later I would learn: one of those pillows you put on your bed so you can sit up at night reading. A handheld battery-operated fan—but not the batteries. A ceramic animal—a hedgehog or something along those lines—with grooved sides where you scattered seeds that you kept moist until, after a while, they sprouted and the animal would be covered with leaves. It's like a pet, she said, only you don't have to worry about cleaning out the cage.

Hamster food, I had reminded her. We needed that too.

I was engrossed in an issue of *Cosmopolitan* that had caught my eye—an article called "What Women Wish Men Knew That They Don't"—when the man leaned over and spoke to me. He was standing in front of the section right next to the puzzles, which was magazines about knitting and gardening. You wouldn't think a person who looked the way he did would want to read about these things. He wanted to talk to me.

I wonder if you could give me a hand here, he said.

This was where I looked at him. He was a tall person. You could see the muscles on his neck and the part of his arms that wasn't covered by his shirt. He had one of those faces where you can tell what the skull would look like with the skin gone, even though the person's still alive. He was wearing the kind of shirt that workers wear at Pricemart—red, with a name on the pocket. Vinnie—and when I looked at him closer, I saw that his leg was bleeding, to the point where some of the blood had soaked through his pants leg onto his shoe, which was actually more like a slipper.

You're bleeding, I said.

I fell out a window. He said it the way a person would if all that happened to him was he got a mosquito bite. Maybe this was why, at the time, this didn't seem like such an odd remark. Or maybe it was that everything seemed so odd back then, this comment in particular didn't stand out.

We should get help, I told him. I was guessing my mother would not be the best one to ask, but there were many other shoppers here. It felt good, him choosing me, out of everyone. This wasn't usually how things went.

I wouldn't want to upset anyone, he said. A lot of people get scared when they see blood. They think they're going to catch some kind of virus, you know, he said.

I understood what he meant, from an assembly we had back in the spring. This was in the days when all people knew was, don't touch anybody else's blood, it could kill you.

You came here with that woman over there, right? he said. He was looking in the direction of my mother, who was standing in the garden section now, looking at a hose. We didn't have one, but we didn't have a garden to speak of either.

Good-looking woman, he said.

My mom.

What I wanted to ask is, if you think she'd give me a ride. I'd be careful not to get blood on your seat. If you could take me someplace. She looks like the type of person who would help me, he said.

It may or may not have been a good thing about my mother that this was true.

Where do you want to go? I asked him. I was thinking, they weren't very considerate to their workers at this store, if when they got injured like this, they had to ask the customers to give them a hand.

Your house?

He said it like a question first, but then he had looked at me like he was a character in *The Silver Surfer*, with superpowers. He put a hand on my shoulder, tight.

Frankly, son, I need this to happen.

I looked at him closer then. He did this thing with his jaw that made you know he was in pain, just trying not to show it—clenched down tight, like he was chewing on a nail. The blood on his pants wasn't that obvious, because they were navy blue. And even though the store was air-conditioned, he was sweating a lot. Now I could see there was a thin trickle of blood coming down the side of his head too, and clotted in his hair.

They had a closeout on baseball caps. Once he'd picked up one of those and put it on his head, you couldn't see the blood much. He was limping badly, but plenty of people did that. He took a fleece vest off the rack and put it over his red Pricemart shirt. I gathered, from the fact that he pulled off the tag, that he wasn't planning on paying for it. Maybe they had some kind of policy for employees.

Just a second, he said. There's one more thing I want to pick up here. Wait here.

You never knew how my mother was going to react to things. There could be some guy going door-to-door with religious pamphlets, and she'd yell at him to go away, but other times I'd come home from school and there'd be this person sitting on our couch having coffee with her.

This is Mr. Jenkins, she said. He wanted to tell us about an orphanage in Uganda he's raising money for, where the children only get to eat once a day and they don't have money to buy pencils. For twelve dollars a month we could sponsor this little boy, Arak. He could be your pen pal. Like a brother.

According to my father, I already had a brother, but we both knew Marjorie's son didn't count.

Great, I said. Arak. She wrote out the check. He gave us a photograph—fuzzy, because it was just a photocopy. She put it on the refrigerator.

There was a woman who wandered into our yard wearing a nightgown one time. This person was very old, and she didn't know where she lived anymore. She kept saying she was looking for her son.

My mother brought her in our house and made her coffee too. I know how confusing things get sometimes, my mother told the woman. We'll straighten this out for you.

Times like this, my mother took charge, and I liked it, how normal she seemed then. After the coffee, and some toast, we had buckled the old woman into the front seat of our car—in fact, this might have been the last time my mother had driven it until now—and cruised around the neighborhood with her for a long time.

You just let me know if anything looks familiar, Betty, my mother told her.

For once, her slow driving made sense, because a man had spotted us, spotted Betty in the front seat, and waved us over.

We were going crazy trying to find her, he said, when my mother rolled the window down. I'm so grateful to you for taking care of her.

She's fine, my mother said. We had the nicest visit. I hope you'll bring her over again.

I like that girl, Betty had said, as the son came around the other side and unbuckled the seat belt. That's the kind of girl you should have married, Eddie. Not that bitch.

I had studied the man's face then, just to check. He was certainly not handsome, but he looked like the kind of person who would be nice. For a second I wished there was a way of telling him my mother wasn't married to anyone anymore. It was just the two of us. He could come over with Betty sometime.

Eddie looked nice, I said, after we drove away. Maybe he's divorced too. You never know.

———

My mother was in the hardware section when we caught up with her. Now that we're here, she said, I should pick up lightbulbs.

This was good news. When a lightbulb burned out at our house, more often than not it just stayed that way. Lately, our house had been getting steadily darker. In the kitchen now, there was only one bulb left that still worked, and not a bright one. Sometimes, at night, if you wanted to see something, you had to open the refrigerator just to shine a little light.

I don't know how we'll manage to get these into the sockets, she said. I can't reach those fixtures in the ceiling.

That was when I introduced the bleeding man. Vinnie. I thought the fact that he was tall would be a plus.

My mother, Adele, I said.

I'm Frank, he said.

Not the first time a person wasn't who you thought they were in this world. Just wearing the wrong shirt, evidently.

You have a good boy here, Adele, he told her. He was kind enough to offer me a ride. Maybe I could repay the favor by giving you a hand with those.

He indicated the lightbulbs.

And anything else you might need done around the house, he said. Not many jobs I can't handle.

She studied his face then. Even with the hat on, you could see some dried blood on his cheek, but she didn't seem to notice that part, or maybe if she did, it didn't seem important.

We went out through the checkout together. He explained to my mother that he was paying for my puzzle book, though he would have to give me an IOU, since at the moment his funds were limited. Evidently he wasn't mentioning the baseball cap and the fleece vest to the cashier.

In addition to my new clothes and the garden hose, and the pillow and the ceramic hedgehog and the lightbulbs and fan, my mother had picked up one of those plywood paddles, with a ball attached on a piece of elastic, that you try to hit as many times in a row as you can.

I thought I'd get you a treat, Henry, she said, laying the toy on the conveyor belt.

I wasn't going to bother explaining that I hadn't played with something like that since I was around six, but Frank spoke up. A boy like this needs a real baseball, he said. Here was the surprising part: he had one in his pocket. Price tag still visible.

I suck at baseball, I told him.

Maybe you used to, he said. He fingered the stitches on the ball and looked at it hard, like what he had in his hand was the whole world.

On the way out, Frank picked up one of those flyers they gave out, featuring that week's specials. When we got to the car, he spread this out on the backseat. I don't want to get blood on your upholstery, Adele, he said. If I can call you that.

Other people's mothers would have asked him a lot of questions probably. Or not taken him in the first place, more likely. My mother just drove. I was wondering if he was going to get into trouble for leaving work that way without telling anyone, but if so, Frank didn't appear to be worried about it.

Of the three of us, it seemed as if I was the only one who felt concerned, actually. I had a feeling I should be doing something about the situation, but as usual, didn't know what. And Frank seemed so calm and clear about things, you wanted to go along with him. Even though really, he was going along with us, of course.

I have a sixth sense when it comes to people, he told my mother. I took one look around that store, big as it was, and knew you were the one.

I won't lie to you, he said. It's a difficult situation. Many people would not want to have anything to do with me at this point. I'm going on my instincts here that you are a very understanding person.

The world is not an easy place to get along, he said. Sometimes you just need to stop everything, sit down and think. Collect your thoughts. Lie low for a bit.

I looked at my mother then. We were coming down Main Street now, past the post office and the drugstore, the bank, the library. All the old familiar places, though in all the times I'd passed this way before, it was never in the company of anyone like Frank. He was pointing out to my mother now that it sounded as if the rotors on her brakes might be a little thin. If he could get his hands on a few tools, he'd like to take a look at that for her, he said.

In the seat next to her, I studied my mother's face, to see if her expression changed, when Frank said these things. I could feel my heart beating, and a tightness in my chest—not fear exactly, but something close, though oddly pleasurable. I had it when my father took Richard and the baby and me, and Marjorie, to Disney World, and we got into our seats on the Space Mountain ride—all of us but Marjorie and the baby. Partly I wanted to get out before the ride started, but then they turned out the lights and this music started and Richard had poked me and said, If you have to barf, just do it in the other direction.

Today is my lucky day, Frank said. Yours too, maybe.

I knew right then, things were about to change. We were headed into Space Mountain now, into a dark place where the ground might give way, and you wouldn't even be able to tell anymore where this car was taking you. We might come back. We might not.

If this had occurred to my mother, she didn't let on. She just held the wheel and stared straight ahead same as before, all the way home.

Chapter 2

Where we lived then—the town of Holton Mills, New Hampshire—was the kind of place where people know each other's business. They'd notice if you left your grass too long between one lawn mowing and the next, and if you painted your house some color besides white, they might not say anything to your face, but they'd talk about it. Where my mother was the kind of person who just wanted to be left alone. There had been a time when she loved being up on a stage, with everybody watching her perform, but at this point, my mother's goal was to be invisible, or as close as she could get.

One of the things she said she liked about our house was where it sat, at the end of the street, with no other houses beyond us and a big field in back, opening onto nothing but woods. Cars hardly ever came by, except on those occasions where someone missed the place they meant to go and had to turn around. Other than people like the man raising money for the orphanage, and the occasional religious types, or someone with a petition, hardly anyone ever came to see us, which to my mother was good news.

It used to be different. We used to visit people's houses sometimes and invite people to ours. But by this point, my mother was down to basically one friend, and even that one hardly ever came by anymore. Evelyn.

My mother and Evelyn met up around the time my father left, when my mother had this idea to start a creative movement class for children at our house—the sort of activity it would have been hard to picture her getting into, later. She actually did things like put up flyers around town and buy an ad in the local paper. The idea was, mothers would come over with their children, and my mother would put on music, and lay out things like scarves and ribbons, and everyone would dance around. When it was over, they'd all have a snack. And if she got enough customers, she wouldn't have to worry about going out into the world and getting a more normal type of job, which wasn't her style.

She went to a lot of effort setting things up for this. She sewed little mats for everyone, and cleared out all the living room furniture, which wasn't all that much to start with, and she bought a rug for the floor that was supposed to be someone's wall-to-wall carpet only they hadn't paid.

I was pretty young at the time, but I remember the morning of the first class, she lit candles to put around the room, and she baked cookies—a health food kind, with whole wheat flour and honey instead of sugar. I didn't want to be in the class, so she told me I could be the one to work the record player and keep an eye on the younger children, if she was busy with one of the older ones, and later, I'd serve the snack. We had a dry run, the morning of her first class, where she showed me what to do and reminded me, if anyone needed to go to the bathroom, to help the little kids with things like fastening their pants after.

Then it was the time her customers were supposed to start showing up. Then it was past the time, and still nobody.

Maybe half an hour after the class was supposed to begin, this woman arrived with a boy in a wheelchair. This was Evelyn and her son, Barry. From the size of him, I got the impression he was probably around my age, but he couldn't talk so much as he just made noises at unusual moments, as if he was watching a movie nobody else could see, and all of a sudden there was a funny part, or one time, it was as if some character in this movie that he really liked a lot had died, because he put his head in his hands—which wasn't all that easy, since his hands jerked around a lot, and so did his head, not necessarily in the same direction— and he just sat there in his chair, making these sobbing sounds.

Evelyn must have had the idea that creative movement could be a good thing for Barry, though if you asked me, he moved pretty creatively to begin with. My mother made a big effort, though. She and Evelyn got Barry on one of the special mats, and she put on a record she liked—the sound track of *Guys and Dolls*— and showed Barry and Evelyn these motions to make to "Luck Be a Lady Tonight." Evelyn showed some promise, she said. But moving to a beat definitely wasn't Barry's type of concept.

The class folded after that one session, but Evelyn and my mother got to be friends. She'd bring Barry over a lot in his oversized stroller, and my mother would make a pot of coffee, and Evelyn would park Barry on the back porch and my mother would tell me to play with him, while Evelyn talked and smoked cigarettes, and my mother listened. Every now and then I'd hear some phrase like *delinquent child support* or face *his responsibilities* or *my cross to bear* or *deadbeat bum*—this was Evelyn talking, never my mother—but mostly I learned to tune the whole thing out.

I tried to think up things Barry could do, games that might interest him, but this was a challenge. One time when I was really bored, I hit on the idea of talking to him in a made-up language—just sounds and noises, along the lines of the ones he made himself now and then. I parked myself in front of his stroller and talked to him that way, using hand gestures, as if I was telling this elaborate story.

This seemed to get Barry excited. At least, he responded by making more sounds than before. He was hooting and yelling, and waving his arms more wildly than normal, which caused my mother and Evelyn to come out on the porch, checking things out.

What's going on here? Evelyn said. From the look on her face, I knew she wasn't happy. She had rushed over to where Barry's wheelchair was parked, and she was smoothing his hair down.

I can't believe you'd let your son make fun of Barry like this, Evelyn told my mother. She was packing up Barry's stuff, collecting her cigarettes. I thought you were the one person who understood, she said.

They were just playing, my mother said. No harm done. Henry's a kind person, really.

But Evelyn and Barry were already out the door.

After that, we hardly ever saw the two of them anymore, which wasn't such a loss in my opinion, except that I knew how lonely my mother was for a friend. After Evelyn, there was nobody.

One time a kid in my class, Ryan, invited me for a sleepover. He was new in town and hadn't figured out yet that I wasn't somebody people had over to their houses, so I said yes. When his dad came to pick me up, I was all ready for a quick getaway, with my toothbrush and my underwear for the next day in a grocery bag.

I think I should introduce myself to your parents first, Ryan's dad said, when I started getting in the car. So they won't worry.

Parent, I said. It's just my mom. And she's OK about this already.

I'll just duck my head in and say hi, he said.

I don't know what she said, but when he came back out, he looked like he felt sorry for me.

You can come over to our house anytime, son, he said to me. But that was the only time I ever did.

So it was a big deal, bringing Frank home in the car with us this way. He was probably the first person we'd had over in a year. Possibly two.

You'll have to excuse the mess, my mother said, as we pulled into the driveway. We've been busy.

I looked at her. Busy with what?

She swung open the door. Joe the hamster was spinning in his wheel. On the kitchen table, a newspaper from several weeks back. Post-it notes taped to the furniture with Spanish words for things written in Sharpie: *Mesa. Silla. Agua. Basura.* Along with teaching herself the dulcimer, learning Spanish had been one of my mother's projects planned to occupy us over the summer. She had started out back in June playing the tapes she got from the library. *¿Dónde está el baño? ¿Cuánto cuesta el hotel?*

The tapes were intended for travelers. What's the point of this? I had asked her, wishing we could just turn on the radio, listen to music, instead. We weren't going to any Spanish-speaking country that I knew of. Just getting to the supermarket every six weeks or so was an accomplishment.

You never know what opportunities might lie ahead, she said.

Now it turned out there was another way for new things to happen. You didn't have to go someplace for the adventure. The adventure came to you.

Inside our kitchen now, with its hopeful yellow walls and its one remaining working lightbulb, and last year's magic ceramic seed-growing animal, a pig, whose crop of green sprouts had long since turned brown and dried up.

Frank looked around slowly. He took in the room as if there was nothing unusual about coming into a kitchen in which a stack of fifty or sixty cans of Campbell's tomato soup lined one wall, like a super-market display in a ghost town, alongside an equally tall stack of boxes containing elbow macaroni, and jars of peanut butter, and bags of raisins. The footprints my mother had painted on the floor from last summer's project of teaching me how to fox-trot and do the two-step were still visible. The idea was for me to put my feet over the foot patterns she'd stenciled on the floor, while she counted out the beats as my partner.

It's a great thing when a man knows how to dance, she said. When a man can dance, the world is his oyster.

Nice place, Frank said. Homey. Mind if I sit down at the *mesa*?

What do you take in your coffee? she asked. She took hers black. Sometimes it seemed as if this was all she lived on. The soup and noodles were bought with me in mind.

Frank studied the headline on the newspaper that sat there, though it was several weeks old. Nobody seemed in a rush to say anything more then, so I thought I'd break the ice.

How did you hurt your leg? I asked him. There was also the question of what happened to his head, but I thought I'd take things one at a time.

I'm going to be straight with you here, Henry, he said. I was surprised he'd taken in my name. To my mother he said, Cream and sugar, thanks, Adele.

Her back was to the two of us, counting out the scoops. He appeared to be speaking to me, or about to, but his eyes were on my mother, and for the first time I could imagine how a person who wasn't her son might see her.

Your mom looks like Ginger on that show on Nickelodeon, *Gilligan's Island*, a girl, Rachel, told me one time. This was in fifth grade, when my mother had put in a rare appearance at my school to watch a production of *Rip Van Winkle* where I played Rip. Rachel had put forward the theory that maybe my mother actually was the actress who played Ginger, and we were living here in this town so she could escape her fans, and the stresses of Hollywood.

At the time, I wasn't sure if I wanted to discourage this theory. It seemed like a better reason than the real one for why my mother hardly ever went anyplace. Whatever the real reason was for that.

Even though she was a mother—not just *a* mother but *my* mother—and what she had on was an old skirt and a leotard she'd had for a million years, I could see now how a person might think she was good-looking. More than that. Most people's mothers you saw at school, parked outside at three o'clock to pick up their kids or running in to bring the homework they'd forgotten, had lost their shape somewhere along the line, from having babies probably. This had happened to my dad's wife, Marjorie, even though, as my mother always pointed out, she was a younger woman.

My mother still had her figure. I knew from one time when she'd tried them on for me that my mother still fit in her old dancing outfits, and though the only place she danced now was our kitchen, she still had dancer's legs. Now Frank was looking at them.

I'm not going to lie to you, he said, again, the words coming out slowly, as his eyes took her in. She was filling the pot on the Mr. Coffee with water now. Maybe she knew he was watching. She was taking her time.

For a minute then, Frank seemed not to be in the room at all, but someplace far away. To look at him, you might think he was watching a movie projected on a screen located somewhere in the vicinity of our refrigerator, that still displayed the faded photocopy of

my African pen pal, Arak, held up by a couple of mag-
nets with calendars on them of years that were over.
Frank's eyes were fixed on some spot in outer space
was how it seemed for a moment then, instead of what
was there in the room, which was just me, at the table,
flipping through my comic book, and my mother, making the coffee.

I hurt my leg, he said—my leg, and my head—from
jumping out a second-floor window at a hospital they'd
taken me to get my appendix out.

At the prison, he said. That's how I got out.

Some people make all these explanations first when
they give you the answer to a question that might not
reflect so well on them (a question like, where do you
work, and the answer is McDonald's, only first they
say something like I'm really an actor or I'm actually
applying to medical school soon; or they try to make
the facts seem different from how they really are, like
saying I'm in sales when what they mean is, they're one
of those people who calls you up on the phone trying
to get you to sign up for an introductory subscription
to the newspaper).

Not Frank, when he told us the news. The state
penitentiary, over in Stinchfield, he said. He lifted
up his shirt then, to reveal a third wound that you
wouldn't have known about otherwise, though this one

was bandaged. The place where they had removed his appendix. Recently, from the looks of it.

My mother turned around to face him. She was holding the coffeepot in one hand and a mug in the other. She poured a thin stream of coffee into it. She set the powdered milk on the table, and the sugar.

We don't have cream, she said.

No worries, he told her.

You escaped? I asked him. So now the police are looking for you? I was scared, but also excited. I knew that finally, something was going to happen in our life. Could be bad, could be terrible. One thing was for certain: it would be different.

I would have gotten farther, he said, except for the damn leg. I couldn't run. Someone had spotted me and they were closing in when I ducked in that store I found you at. That's where they lost my trail, out in the parking lot.

Frank was scooping the sugar into his coffee now. Three spoonfuls. I'd be grateful if you'd let me sit here awhile, he said. It would be hard going back out there right now. I did some damage when I landed.

This was one thing the two of them could agree on—my mother and Frank: that it was hard going out into the world.

I wouldn't ask anything of you, he said. I'd try to help out. I never intentionally hurt anyone in my life.

You can stay here awhile, my mother said. I just can't let anything happen to Henry.

The boy has never been in better hands, Frank told her.

Chapter 3

My mother was a good dancer. More than that. The way she danced, she could have been in a movie, if they still made movies where people did that kind of dancing, which they didn't. But we had videos of a few of them, and she knew some of the routines. *Singin' in the Rain,* the part where the man twirls around a lamppost from being in love, and the girl's wearing a raincoat. My mother did that number one time, in the middle of Boston, back when we still went places sometimes. She took me to the science museum, and just when we got out it started to pour and there was this lamppost, and she just started dancing. Later, when she did things like that, I'd feel embarrassed. Back then, I was just proud.

Dancing was how she met my father. Whatever else she had to say about him, she told me the man knew how to move a woman around the dance floor, which meant a lot in her book. I couldn't remember all that much about times my parents were still together, but I could remember the dancing part, and young as I was I understood they were the best.

Some men just set their hand on your shoulder or against the small of your back, she said. The good ones know, there has to be strong pressure there. Something to push back against.

How to hold your partner when ballroom dancing was only one of the things my mother had a strong opinion about. She also believed that microwave ovens gave you cancer and sterility, which was why—though we had one—she made me promise I'd hold a cookbook over my crotch if I was ever in the kitchen at my father's house when Marjorie was heating something up.

One time she had a dream that a freak tsunami was going to hit the state of Florida shortly, which was clear evidence that I should not go on the Disney trip with my father and Marjorie—never mind the fact that Orlando was situated inland. She decided that our next-door neighbor, Ellen Farnsworth, had been enlisted by my father to collect information to support his custody case. How else could you explain the fact that one day after my father had called up to demand that my mother take me to Little League tryouts,

Mrs. Farnsworth had stopped over to ask if I wanted a ride. Why else would she come over to ask if we had an extra egg, with the excuse that she'd run out in the middle of making chocolate chip cookies? She just wanted to check up on us, my mother said. Gather incriminating information.

I wouldn't put it past that woman to have bugged our house, she said. They make microphones so small now, there could be one hidden in this saltshaker.

Hello, Ellen, she called out, over the salt, her voice almost musical. There had been a time when I was in awe of how she knew things like this, and how, once she found them out, she knew just what to do about them. I didn't feel that way anymore.

As for the Little League tryouts: Little League was just one of those organizations where they squelch children's creativity by making them follow all these rules, my mother said.

Like how they only let people get three strikes? I asked her. Like how the team with the most runs wins?

I was being a wise guy of course. I hated baseball, but sometimes I also hated how my mother looked at everything other people did, looking for the reason it wouldn't be our kind of thing. And why they weren't our kind of people.

What is it with that woman, anyway? she said, right after Mrs. Farnsworth had her fourth child. Every time I turn around she's having another baby.

These were the kinds of topics we talked about when we ate dinner. She talked about them. I listened. My mother didn't believe the television set should be on when people were having dinner. There should be conversation. In the kitchen, under the light of our one remaining bulb, while we ate our frozen dinner (heated in the oven, never a microwave), she discussed the possibility that the Farnsworths' birth control method must be faulty—diaphragm perhaps?—and told me the stories from her life, though only about the old days. This is where I learned everything: when she set the tray down, after she poured her wine.

Your father was a very handsome man, she told me. Same as you will be. She had mailed a picture of him to someone in Hollywood one time, back when they were first married, because she thought he could be a movie star.

They never wrote back, she said. She seemed surprised.

My father was the one who came from this town. She'd met him at the wedding of a girl she went to school with, down in Massachusetts, the North Shore.

I don't even know why Cheryl invited me, she said. We weren't that good friends. But you could count me in anytime I knew there was dancing.

My father had come to this wedding with someone else. My mother came alone, but she liked it that way. That way, she said, you don't get stuck all night with someone, if they don't know how to dance.

My father did. By the end of the evening, people had opened up a spot on the dance floor just for the two of them. He was leading her in moves she hadn't done before, like a round-the-world flip that made her glad she'd worn her red underpants.

He was a very good kisser. After they met, they'd stayed in bed all that weekend, and for the first three days of the week following. I didn't necessarily need to hear all the things my mother told me, but this never stopped her. By the second glass of wine, she wasn't really talking to me at all anymore, she was just talking.

If we could have just danced all the time, she said. If we never had to stop dancing, everything would have been fine.

She quit her job at the travel agency and moved in with him. He wasn't selling insurance yet. He had this wagon he drove around, selling hot dogs at fairs, and popcorn. She got to go around with him, and at night, they didn't even come back to his apartment sometimes, if they'd driven up north someplace, or to the ocean. They kept a sleeping bag under the seat. One was enough.

This was strictly summer work, of course, she said. Winter came, they headed south to Florida. She got a job for a while, serving margaritas at a bar in Fort Lauderdale. He sold hot dogs at the beach. Nighttime, they went dancing.

I tried to eat slowly when my mother told these stories. I knew when the meal was over, she'd remember where we were and get up from the table. When she talked about their old days, the Florida days, and the hot-dog wagon, and the plans they had to drive out to California sometime and try out to be dancers on some TV variety show, something happened to her face, the way people get when a song comes on the radio that used to play when they were young, or they see a dog go down the street that reminds them of the one they used to have when they were a kid—a Boston terrier maybe, or a collie. For a moment, she looked like my grandmother, the day she heard Red Skelton died, and like herself, the day my father had pulled up in front of our house with the baby in his arms, that he called my sister. He'd been gone over a year by the time that happened, but that moment when she saw the baby—that was the worst.

I forgot how little babies were, she said, after he'd left. There was that melted look on her face then too. Maybe the word is *crumpled*. Then she recovered. You were much cuter, she said.

Back when she used to take me places, she also told me stories while she drove, but once she started staying home all the time, dinners were when she told me her stories, and even when they were sad I never wanted them to end. I always knew, after I set my fork down, the story was over, or even if it hadn't ended—because these weren't stories with endings—and her face changed back.

We'd better clear away these dishes, she said. You have homework to do.

The real ending came when my parents moved back north and sold the hot-dog wagon. They didn't have that kind of show on TV anymore, like when we were growing up, she said. With dancers. They had driven all the way across the country without ever noticing that *The Sonny and Cher Show* and *The Glen Campbell Hour* had been canceled. But that was just as well, actually, because what she wanted most was never to be some dancer on television. She wanted to have a baby.

Then you were on the way, she said. And my dream came true.

My father got the job selling insurance policies. His specialty was injury and disability. Nobody could calculate faster than my father how much money a person got for losing an arm, or an arm and a leg, or two legs, or the bonanza, all four limbs, which, if they were smart enough to have bought a policy from him before, meant they were a millionaire, set up for life.

My mother had stayed home with me after that. They lived with my father's mother then, and after she died, they got the house, though that was not the place we lived after the divorce. My father lived in our old house with Marjorie now, and Richard, and Chloe. He took out a second mortgage on that one, to buy my mother out, which was the money my mother used to get the place we moved into. Smaller, without the tree in the yard where my swing had been set up, but enough room for how our family was now, the two of us.

These were not stories she told me over dinner. This part I had pieced together on my own, and from Saturday nights with my father, when he and Marjorie took me out to dinner, and sometimes he said things like, If your mother hadn't made me give her all that money for the house, or Marjorie would press her lips together and ask me if my mother had applied for a normal job yet.

My mother's problem about leaving the house had been going on so long now I couldn't remember when it started. But I knew what she thought: it was a bad idea, going out in the world.

It was about the babies, she said. All those crying babies everywhere, and the mothers stuffing pacifiers in their mouths. She said more too—about weather and traffic, and nuclear power plants and the danger of waves from high-voltage lines. But it was the babies that got to her most, and their mothers.

They never pay attention, she said. It's as if the big accomplishment was giving birth to these children, and once they had them, the whole thing was just a chore that you got through the best you could by pumping them full of soda and sitting them down in front of videos (these were just starting to get popular then). Doesn't anyone ever talk to their children anymore? she said.

Well, she did, all right. Too much, in my opinion. She was always home now. The only person she really had any interest in seeing now, she said, was me.

Now and then we'd still drive places, but instead of going in herself she'd send me with the money and stay in the car. Or she'd say why bother driving to the store when you can order from Sears? When we did go to the supermarket, she'd stock up on things like Campbell's soup and Cap'n Andy fish dinners, peanut butter and frozen waffles, and pretty soon it was like we lived in a bomb shelter. Sears had already provided the deep freeze by this point, and it was filled with frozen dinners. A hurricane could have hit, and we'd be set for weeks, we had so many provisions stored up. Powdered milk was better for me anyway, she said. Less fat. Her parents had both suffered from high cholesterol and died young. We had to keep an eye on that.

Then she started getting everything from mail-order catalogs—this being the days before the Internet—even things like our underwear and socks, and commenting on how much traffic there was in town now, that a person really shouldn't even drive there anymore, especially when you considered how it contributed to pollution. I had this idea we should get a motor scooter: I'd seen a character riding one on a TV show, and I pictured how much fun it could be, the two of us buzzing around town, doing our errands.

How many errands does a person really need to do? she said. When you think about it, all that going around to places just wasted so much time you could be spending in your own home.

Back when I was younger, I was always trying to get her out of the house. Let's go bowling, I said. Miniature golf. The science museum. I tried to think of things she might like—a Christmas craft show over at the high school, a production of *Oklahoma!* put on by the Lions Club.

There'll be dancing, I said. Big mistake, to mention this.

They just call it dancing, she said.

Sometimes I wondered if the problem was how much she'd loved my father. I had heard about cases where a person loved someone so much that if they died or went away, the person never got over it. This was what people meant when they talked about a broken heart. Once, when we were having our frozen dinners, and she'd just poured herself a third glass of wine, I had considered asking my mother about this. I wondered if what it took to make a person hate another person the way she seemed to hate my father now was having once loved him in equal measure. It seemed like something they might teach you in science class— physics, though we hadn't studied this yet. Like a teeter-totter where how high the person goes up on one side depends on how low the person goes down on the other.

What I decided was, it hadn't been losing my father that broke my mother's heart, if that was what had taken place, as it appeared. It was losing love itself— the dream of making your way across America on popcorn and hot dogs, dancing your way across America, in a sparkly dress with red underpants. Having someone think you were beautiful, which, she had told me, my father used to tell her she was, every day.

Then there's nobody saying that anymore, and you are like one of those ceramic hedgehogs with the plants growing on it that the person who bought it forgot to keep watered. You are like a hamster nobody remembered to feed.

That was my mother. I could try to make up for some of the neglect, which I did, when I left her notes on her bed that said things like "For the World's Number One Mom" with some rock I found or a flower, and jokes from my joke-a-day book, times when I made up funny songs for her, or cleaned out the silverware drawer and laid shelf liner paper on all the shelves, and when her birthday came around, or Christmas, and I gave her coupon books with the pages stapled together and on each one a promise like "Redeemable for carrying out trash," or "Good for one vacuuming job." When I was younger, I had made a coupon once that said "Husband for a day," with the promise that whenever she cashed that one in, it would be just like having a husband around the house again, whatever she wanted, I'd take care of it.

At the time I was too young to understand the part of being Husband for a Day I was not equipped to carry out, but in another way I think I sensed my own terrible inadequacy and it was the knowledge of this that weighed on me, when I lay in my narrow bed in my small room, next to hers, the walls between us so thin it was almost as if she were there with me. I could feel her loneliness and longing, before I had a name for it. It had probably never been about my father really. Looking at him now, it was hard to imagine he could ever have been worthy of her. What she had loved was loving.

A year or two after the divorce, on one of our Saturday nights, my father had asked me if I thought my mother was going crazy. I was probably seven or eight at the time, not that my being older would have made it any easier to address this question. I was old enough to know that most people's mothers didn't sit in the car while their son ran into the grocery store with the money, to do the shopping for them, or go up to the teller at the bank—no ATM machines yet—with a check for five hundred dollars. Enough cash, she said, so we wouldn't have to make another trip for a long time.

I had been to other people's houses, so I knew how other mothers were—the way they went to jobs and drove their children around and sat on the benches at the ball games and went to the beauty parlor and the mall and attended back-to-school night. They had friends, not just one sad woman with a retarded son in an oversize stroller.

She's just shy, I told my father. She's busy with her music lessons. This was the year my mother had taken up the cello. She had watched a documentary about a famous cello player, possibly the greatest in the world, who got a disease so she started missing notes and dropping the bow and pretty soon she couldn't play anymore, and her husband, who was also a famous musician, had left her for another woman.

My mother had told me this story while we finished our Cap'n Andy frozen fish dinners one night. The husband had started sleeping with the famous cello player's sister, my mother told me. After a while, the cello player couldn't walk anymore. She had to lie there in bed, in the same house where the husband was in bed with the sister.

Making love in the next room. What do you think of that, Henry? my mother had said.

Bad, I said. Not that she was really waiting for my answer.

My mother was learning to play the cello as a tribute to Jacqueline du Pré, she told me. She didn't have a teacher, but she rented a cello from a music store a couple of towns over. A little on the small side, because it was meant for a child, but good enough to start on. Once she got the hang of it, she could move up to something better.

My mom is fine, I told my father. She just gets sad sometimes, when people die. Like Jacqueline du Pré.

You could come live with Marjorie and me, he said. And Richard and Chloe. If that was something you wanted, we'd take her to court. They'd have her evaluated.

Mom's great, I said. She's having her friend Evelyn over tomorrow. I get to play with Evelyn's son, Barry.

(*Blah blah goo goo,* I thought. *Booby dooby zo zo.* Barry talk.)

I looked at my father's face as I told him these things. If he had wanted to pursue it, I might have said more—told him who Barry was, and how my mother and Evelyn spent their time when she came over, the plan they had to maybe get a farm in the country together, where they could homeschool their children and grow their own vegetables. Follow a macrobiotic diet to reactivate Barry's brain cells, the ones that didn't work so well at the moment. Run the lights off solar power. Or wind power, or this machine Barry's mother had seen on *Evening Magazine,* where you stored up energy to run your refrigerator by pedaling for an hour every morning on this bicycle-type contraption. Save money on the electric bill and slim down, all at once. Not that my mother needed that, but Evelyn did.

But my father, hearing my report on my mother's busy, happy schedule of activities, had looked relieved, the way I knew he would. I knew he didn't really want me to come live with him and Marjorie, any more than I wanted to go there and live with him and a woman who referred to her two children (and me, when I was with them) as munchkins. Or kidlets, her other favorite term.

Even though I was his real son, and Richard wasn't, Richard was more his type. Richard always got on base when he came up to bat at Little League. Where I sat on the bench, until the day when even my father agreed maybe this wasn't my sport. One thing was for sure: nobody missed me on the Holton Mills Tigers after I quit.

I just asked because I get the impression she's depressed, my father said. And I wouldn't want you suffering through some kind of traumatic experience there. I want you to have someone around who can take care of you properly.

My mom takes care of me great, I said. We do fun things all the time. People come over. We have hobbies.

We're learning Spanish, I told him.

Chapter 4

They were looking for him all over town of course. Frank. We only got one channel on our TV, but even before the regular news came on at six, they interrupted the program to tell about it. The theory was that, given his injuries, and the fact that the police had roadblocks up within an hour of his escape—and in our town, there was basically only one road in and one out—he could not have gone far.

There was his face on the screen. It was funny, seeing this person on your TV who was also sitting in your living room. Like how that girl Rachel might have felt if she was over at my house, which she never would be, and a rerun of *Gilligan's Island* came on just at the moment my mother came into the room with a plate of cookies for us, which was also not happening, and she still believed my mother was actually that actress.

"We have a celebrity in our midst," Marjorie had said the night she and my dad took me out for a sundae after my performance as Rip Van Winkle. Only this time it would have been real.

Now they were interviewing the head of the Highway Patrol, who said the escaped man had been spotted over at the shopping plaza. They were calling Frank dangerous, possibly armed, though we knew he wasn't. I'd already asked him if he had a gun. When he told me no, I was disappointed.

If you see this individual, contact the authorities immediately, the anchorwoman said. Then a phone number flashed on the screen. My mother didn't write it down.

Evidently he'd had his appendix surgery the day before. They said something about how he'd tied up the nurse who was supposed to be watching him and jumped out a window, but we knew that part already, and we also knew he'd let the nurse go before he got out the window. They had her on-screen now, saying how he'd always been thoughtful and considerate with her. A good patient, though it had definitely come as a shock when he tied her up that way. In my mother's eyes, this probably made him seem more trustworthy, knowing he hadn't changed his story for us.

The other thing they said on the news was what he was in for. Murder.

Up until then, Frank hadn't said anything. We were all just watching together, like this was *Evening Magazine* or some other show that came on at that hour. But when they said the part about how he'd killed somebody, you could see this place in his jaw twitch.

They never explain the details, he said. It didn't happen the way they're going to say it did.

On the television, they had gone back to regular programming now. A rerun of *Happy Days.*

Adele, I need to ask if I can stay with you two for a period of time, Frank said. They'll have a search out on all the highways and trains and buses. The one thing nobody expects is me sticking around.

It wasn't my mother who pointed out this next part. It was me. I didn't want to mention it, because I liked him, and I didn't want to make him mad, but it seemed important for someone to bring this up.

Isn't it against the law to harbor a criminal? I asked him, a fact I'd picked up from watching television. Then I felt bad that I'd used that word. Even though we hardly knew Frank at this point, it seemed mean to call this person who had bought me a puzzle book, and put in new lightbulbs all over the house, a criminal. He had complimented the color my mother had chosen to paint the kitchen—this certain shade of yellow that he said reminded him of buttercups on his grandma's farm when he was growing up. He had told us we'd never eaten chili like he was going to make for us.

You have a wise son here, Adele, Frank told her. It's good to know he's looking out for you. That's everything a boy should do for his mother.

It would only be a problem if someone found Frank here, my mother said. So long as nobody knows he came by, there's no harm done.

I knew the other part. My mother didn't worry about laws. My mother didn't go to church, but the one who looked after us, she said, was God.

True enough, Frank said. But it's still not acceptable to place you and your family here in jeopardy.

Our family. He spoke of us as a family.

This is why I'm going to tie you up, he said. Only you, Adele. Henry here knows he doesn't want anything to happen to his mother. That's the reason he won't go to the police or call anyone. I'm correct on this, right, Henry?

My mother, hearing this, did not move from her spot on the couch. Nobody said anything for a minute. We could hear the scraping of the wheel in Joe's cage as he pawed his way in circles, the click of his little nails against the metal, and the hiss of the water on the stove from our Meal in Minutes dinner.

I need to ask you to take me up to your bedroom, Adele, he said. I'm guessing a woman like you would have a few scarves. Silk is good. Rope or twine can cut into the skin.

The door was four feet away from me, and still partly open from when we'd carried in the bags from our shopping. Across the street was the Jervises' house, where Mrs. Jervis sometimes called out to me, when I went by on my bike, to comment on the weather. Beyond that, the Farnsworths, and the Edwardses, who had come over one time to ask my mother if she intended to rake our leaves anytime soon, because they'd started blowing onto other people's lawns in the neighborhood. Every December, Mr. Edwards put up so many lights people from other towns drove by to see, which meant they often went by our house that time of year.

People spend all this money putting up lights, my mother said. Did they ever hear of looking at the stars?

I could burst out the door and run to their houses now. I could grab the phone and dial a number. The police. My father. Not my father: he'd use this as evidence that my mother was crazy, the way he always said.

But I didn't want to do this. Maybe Frank had a weapon, maybe he didn't. Evidently he had killed someone. But he didn't seem like a person who would hurt my mother or me.

I studied my mother's face. For once, she actually looked fine. There was a pinkness in her cheeks I wasn't accustomed to, and her eyes were locked on his eyes. Which were blue.

Actually, I have a silk scarf collection, my mother said. They were my mother's.

It's about keeping up appearances, Frank said, in a quiet voice. I think you understand what I mean.

I got up and went to the door. Closed it, so nobody could see inside. I sat there in the living room, with my legs folded under me, and watched the two of them climb the steps up to her room: my mother first, Frank following behind. They seemed to walk slower than normal, climbing those stairs, as if every step required thought. As if there was more at the top than just a bunch of old scarves. As if they weren't even sure what might be up there and they were taking their time now, thinking about it.

After a while, they were back. He asked her which chair she found the most comfortable. Nothing near a window was all.

You could tell from the way he winced now and then that he was still hurting from the injury, not to mention the appendix surgery. Still he could do what he needed to.

He had brushed off the seat first. Ran his hand over the wood, as if he was checking for splinters. Not roughly, but with a firm grip, he put his hands on her shoulders and lowered her onto the seat. He stood over her for a minute, like he was thinking. She looked up, as if she was too. If she was afraid, you wouldn't have known it.

To tie her feet, he'd gotten down on the floor. My mother was wearing the type of shoes she favored, that looked like ballet slippers. He slipped them off her feet—first one, then the other, his hand cradling one arch. He had a surprisingly large hand, or maybe it was just how small her feet were.

I hope you don't mind my saying this, Adele, he said. But you have beautiful toes.

A lot of dancers ruin their feet, my mother said. I was just lucky.

He took one of the scarves from the table then—a pink one, with roses, and another that had some kind of geometric design. It seemed to me he placed this against his cheek but maybe I imagined that part. I know that time seemed to be standing still, or moving so slowly at least that I had no idea how many minutes had passed, when he wrapped the first scarf around her ankle and began to tie. He had attached the chair to a piece of metal that ran under the table, where you could put an extension leaf in for times when you had company over and you needed to make room for more people. Not that we'd ever had to do this.

It seemed as if Frank forgot I was even there as he positioned the scarves—one on each ankle, that he attached to the legs of the chair, one around her wrists, tied to each other in her lap, so that she looked as if she was praying, sitting there. Sitting in church, anyway. Not that we ever went.

Then he seemed to remember me again. I don't want any of this to upset you, son, he said. This is just something a person has to do in these types of situations.

One other thing, he told my mother. I don't want to embarrass you in any way by saying this. But when you feel a need to use the restroom. Or have any intimate need that might require privacy. Just say the word.

I'll just sit myself down beside you if that's all the same with you, he said. Keep an eye on things.

Just for a second, that look came across his face again, where you knew he was hurting.

She asked him about his leg then. My mother wasn't a big believer in medicine, but she kept rubbing alcohol under the sink. She didn't want him to get an infection, she said. And maybe they could rig up some kind of splint for his ankle.

We'll have you back to how you were before you know it, she said.

What if I don't want to be how I was? he said. What if I want to be different now?

He fed her. My hands were free, but because hers were tied, he set the plate in front of himself on the table, but close enough for the fork to reach. And he was right about the chili he made us. The best I ever tasted.

How it was, watching him bring the food to her lips, and watching her take it, was nothing like my mother's friend, Evelyn, when she used to come over with Barry, and she'd give him his meals. Or Marjorie with the baby they called my little sister, spooning the peaches into her mouth while she was talking on the phone or yelling at Richard about something, so at least half of the meal dripped down the front of Chloe's sleeper suit without Marjorie even noticing. You might think it would be a little humiliating for a person, having to sit there like that, relying on this other person to give them their meal. If they put too much on the spoon, you'd have to take it, or too little, you could sit there with your mouth open, begging. You might think this would leave a person feeling mad or desperate, in which case the only thing they could do about it was to spit the food back out at the person who was giving it to them. Then go hungry.

But there was something about the way Frank fed my mother that made the whole thing almost beautiful, like he was a jeweler or a scientist, or one of those old Japanese men who work all day on a single bonsai.

Every spoonful, he made sure it was the right amount, so she wouldn't choke on the food, and none of it would drool over the side of her lips onto her chin. You knew he understood she was the type of person who cared about how she looked, even when she was tied up in her own kitchen with nobody but her son and an escaped prisoner there to see her. Maybe how she looked to her son didn't matter, but the other part did.

Before he lifted the spoon to her mouth, he blew on the chili, to not burn her tongue. Every few spoonfuls, he understood she should have something to drink. This would be water or wine, depending. He alternated those without her having to say which.

Unlike dinners with me, where she was always talking, telling her stories, we ate in near total silence that night. It was as if they didn't need to speak, these two. Their eyes were locked on each other. Still, many things were coming across: the way she arched her neck toward him, like a bird in the nest, the way his body leaned forward in the chair, like a painter in front of a piece of canvas. Sometimes making a brushstroke. Other times, just studying his work.

Partway through the meal, a drop of tomato sauce trickled onto my mother's cheek. She could have licked it off with her own tongue probably, but she must have understood by this point that there would be no need. He dipped his napkin into the glass of water and touched it to her skin. His finger also touched the skin of her cheek then, for a moment, to dry it off. She made a small nodding motion. Easy to miss, but her hair had brushed his hand, and when that happened, he'd taken the strand of hair and brushed it off her face.

He himself did not eat. I had been hungry, but sitting there now, at the table with the two of them, it felt as crude to chew or swallow as it would have to munch on popcorn at a baby's christening, or lick an ice-cream cone while your friend told you his dog died. I shouldn't be here was how I felt.

I guess I'll take my dinner in the living room, I said. Watch some TV.

The telephone was also there of course. I could have picked it up and dialed. The door, the neighbors, the car with the key in it—nothing had changed. I turned on *Three's Company* and ate my chili.

A few shows later, when I got tired, I looked back in the kitchen. The dishes had been cleared away and washed. He had fixed tea, but nobody was drinking any. I could hear the low sound of their voices, though not the words they said.

I called out then that I was going to bed. This was the moment my mother would normally have said "Sweet dreams," but she was occupied.

Chapter 5

My mother didn't have a regular job, but she sold vitamins over the phone to people. Every couple of weeks the company she worked for—MegaMite—sent her a printout with phone numbers of potential customers all around our region, to call up and tell about the product. Every time she sold a vitamin package, the company paid her a commission. We also got a discount on vitamins for ourselves, which was a fringe benefit. She made sure I took my MegaMites twice a day. She could see the results in my eyeballs, she said. Some people had these grayish corneas, but mine were white as an egg, and the other thing she'd noticed already was how, unlike so many other kids my age (not that she saw other kids my age much), I did not suffer from acne.

You are too young to appreciate this yet, she told me, but in the future, you'll be grateful for how the minerals you're taking in now will affect your virility and sexual health. They've done studies on that. Particularly at the moment, as you enter puberty, it's important to consider these things.

These were some of the lines my mother was supposed to deliver to the people on her potential customer printouts, but mostly the person who heard them was me.

My mother was a terrible MegaMite salesperson. She hated calling up strangers, for one thing, so very often she avoided the whole thing. The new printouts would sit on our kitchen table, on top of the old ones, with a name checked off here and there, and the occasional comment—*Line busy. Call back at more convenient time. Wishes she could buy but no $.*

I can tell you're someone who should have these vitamins, Marie, I heard her saying on the phone one time—a rare night when she had set herself up at the table with the phone, and a pen to take notes, and the list of numbers they'd given her. So far so good, I was thinking, when I came into the kitchen to fix myself a bowl of cereal with powdered milk. This was particularly good news to me because at the time she'd promised, if she could drum up another thirty

MegaMite customers, she'd buy me the boxed set of Sherlock Holmes I'd been wanting, from Classics Book Club, that we'd joined the year before to get the free world atlas and a leather-bound edition of *The Chronicles of Narnia* with full-color illustrations.

So here's what I'm going to do, Marie, she was saying now. *I'm going to send you the vitamins anyway. I'll get them myself on my company discount. You can send me a check later, when things improve for you.*

What makes you think that person you never even met is any worse off than us? I asked her.

Because I have you, she said. Marie doesn't.

I don't imagine your father has told you anything about sex, she said one night, when we were having our Cap'n Andy. I had dreaded this moment, and might have avoided it if I'd told her yes, he explained everything, but it was never possible to lie to her.

No, I said.

Most people put all this focus onto the physical changes you'll be going through soon. Maybe they've even started. I don't intend to invade your personal privacy by asking about that.

They explained everything in our health assembly, I told her. Cut her off at the pass was my thought. As swiftly as possible.

They never tell you about love, Henry, she said. For all the discussion of body parts, the one that never gets mentioned is your heart.

That's OK, I said. Desperate to get this conversation finished. Only her words kept on coming.

There is another aspect your health teacher is unlikely to explore. Though he may refer to hormones. No doubt he has done that.

I braced myself for all the horrifying words then. *Ejaculation. Semen. Erection. Pubic hair. Nocturnal emission. Masturbate.*

Desire, she said. People never talk about longing. They act as if making love is all about secretions and body functions and reproduction. They forget to mention how it feels.

Stop, stop, I wanted to say. I wanted to put my hand over her mouth. I wanted to jump up from the table and run out into the night. Mow the lawn, rake leaves, shovel snow, be anyplace but here.

There is another kind of hunger, she said, clearing our plates—hers barely touched, as usual—and pouring herself a glass of wine.

Hunger for the human touch, she said. She sighed deeply then. If there was any doubt before, it was clear. She knew about this one.

Chapter 6

There is a thing that happens sometimes, where you wake up and you forget for a minute what happened the day before. It takes your brain a few seconds to reset, before you remember whatever it was that happened—sometimes good, more often bad— that you knew about when you went to bed the night before and blanked out in the night. I remember the feeling from when my father left, and how, when I'd first opened my eyes the next day, and stared out the window, I knew something was wrong without re- membering exactly what. Then it came to me.

When Joe got out of his cage and for three days we didn't know where he was, and all we could do was scatter hamster food all over the house hoping he'd come out, which he finally did—that was one of those times. When my grandmother died—not because I actually knew her very well, but because my mother had loved her and now she was going to be an orphan, which meant that she would feel even more alone in the world, which meant it was more important than ever for me to stick around and have dinner with her, play cards, listen to her stories, listen to more—that was one of those times.

The morning after we brought Frank home from Pricemart—the Friday before the start of Labor Day weekend—I woke up forgetting he was there. I just knew something was different at our house.

The tip-off came when I smelled coffee. This was not how my mother did it. She was never out of bed this early. There was music coming from the radio. Classical.

Something was baking. Biscuits, it turned out.

It only took a few seconds before I got it. Unlike other times I'd woken up and then remembered some piece of news, there was no bad feeling to this one. I remembered the silk scarves now, the woman on TV saying the word *murderer*. Still, the feeling I had, when I thought of Frank, contained no fear. More like anticipation and excitement. It was as if I'd been in the middle of a book that I had to put down when I got too tired to keep reading, or a video put on pause. I wanted to pick back up with the story and find out what happened to the characters, except that the characters were us.

Coming down the stairs, I considered the possibility that my mother would be where she'd been when I left her the night before, tied in the chair, with her own silk scarves. But the chair was empty. The person at the stove was Frank. He had evidently made some kind of splint for his ankle, and he was still limping, but he was getting around.

I would have gone out and got us eggs, he said, but it might not be a great idea stepping into the 7-Eleven at this moment. He nodded in the direction of the newspaper, which he must have picked up from the curb where it had been tossed sometime before the sun came up. Above the fold, next to a headline about the heat wave they were predicting for the holiday weekend, a photograph of a face both familiar and unrecognizable—his. Only the man in the photograph had a hard, mean look and a series of numbers plastered across his chest, where the one in our kitchen had tucked a dishrag into his waistband and wore a potholder.

Eggs would really hit the spot with these biscuits, he said.

We don't go in much around here for perishable groceries, I told him. Our diet mostly featured canned goods and frozen foods.

You've got enough room in back for chickens, he said. Three or four nice little Rhode Island Reds, you could fry yourself up a plate of eggs every morning. A fresh-laid egg is a whole other thing from what you get in those cardboard boxes from the store. Golden yolks. Stand right up off the plate like a pair of tits on a Las Vegas showgirl. Companionable little buggers too, chickens.

He grew up on a farm, he said. He could set us up. Show me the ropes. I shot a look at the newspaper while he was talking, but I thought if I looked too interested in the story of Frank's escape and the search now on to find him, it might hurt his feelings.

Where's my mom? I asked him. For just a second there, it occurred to me to be worried. Frank hadn't seemed like the type to do anything bad to us, but now a picture flashed through my brain of her in the basement, chained to the oil burner, maybe, with a silk scarf over her mouth instead of wrapped softly around her wrists. In the trunk of our car. In the river.

She needed her sleep, he said. We stayed up real late, talking. But it might be nice if you took her this. Does she like coffee in bed?

How would I know? The question had never come up.

Or maybe we'll just let her catch a few extra winks, he said.

He was taking the biscuits out of the oven now, laying them on a plate, with a cloth napkin on top to keep them warm. Here's a tip for you, Henry, he said. Never slice a biscuit with a knife. You want to pull them apart, so you get all the textures. What you're aiming for is peaks and valleys. Picture a freshly rototilled garden, where the soil is a little uneven. More places for the butter to soak in.

We don't usually keep butter around, I said. We use margarine.

Now that's what I call a crime, Frank said.

He poured himself a cup of coffee. The newspaper was sitting right there, but neither of us reached for it.

I don't blame you for wondering, he told me. Any sensible person would. All I want to tell you is, there's more to this story than you'll see in that paper there.

I had no answer to that one, so I poured myself a glass of orange juice.

You got any plans for the big weekend? he asked. Cookouts, ball games, and whatnot? Looks like it's going to be a scorcher. Good time to head to the beach.

Nothing special, I said. My dad takes me out for dinner Saturdays, that's about it.

What's his story anyway? Frank asked. How does a fellow let a woman like your mother get away?

He got together with his secretary, I said. Even at thirteen, I was aware of the sound of the words as I spoke them, the awful ordinariness of them. It was like admitting you wet your pants, or shoplifted. Not even an interesting story. Just a pathetic one.

No offense intended here, son. But if that's the case, good riddance. A person like that doesn't deserve a woman like her.

It had been a long time since I'd seen my mother looking the way she did when she came into the room that morning. Her hair, that she usually pulled back in a rubber band, was hanging down on her shoulders, and it seemed fluffier than normal, as if she'd slept on a cloud. She had on a blouse I didn't think she'd ever worn before—white, with little flowers all over it, the top button left open. Not so much revealed that she looked cheap—I was still thinking about that line he'd uttered, about the Las Vegas showgirl—but friendly, inviting. She had put on earrings, and lipstick, and when she got closer I could tell she was wearing perfume. Just the faintest whiff of something lemony.

He asked her how she'd slept. Like a baby, she said, then laughed.

I don't know why they say that, actually, she said. Considering how often babies get up in the night.

She asked if he had any children.

One, he said. He'd be nineteen now if he was living. Francis Junior.

Some people, like my stepmother, Marjorie, would have made some kind of sympathetic remark here, about how sorry they were. They would have asked what happened, or if they were religious, said something about how Frank's son was no doubt in a better place now anyway. Or told about someone they knew who had lost a kid. I had been noticing lately, how often people did that: take whatever anybody else mentioned in the way of a problem, and turn it around to them, and their own sorry situation.

My mother, hearing about Frank's son who died, said nothing, but the look on her face changed in such a way that no more was needed for the moment. It was a moment like the one the night before, when he was feeding her the chili, and holding the wineglass up for her to sip from, and I got the feeling they had gotten past normal words and moved on to a whole other language. He knew she felt bad for him. She knew he understood this. Same as when she sat down in the chair at the place he'd set for her—her same chair from the night before—she held her wrists out for him to put the scarves back on. They had an understanding now, the two of them. What I did mostly was watch.

I don't think we'll be needing these, Adele, he said, folding the scarves carefully and setting them on top of a stack of canned tuna. Like how the pope might handle some kind of special garment popes wear, when he puts them away.

I don't plan on using these again, Frank said. But if the day ever comes when you have to say I tied you up, you'll pass the lie detector.

I wanted to ask When was that day? Who would be giving her that test? Where would he be, when she took it? What would they ask me?

My mother nodded. Who taught you to make biscuits like this? she said.

My grandma, he said. After my parents died, she was the one that raised me.

There'd been a car wreck, he told us. It happened when he was seven. Late at night, driving back from a visit with the relatives in Pennsylvania, they hit a patch of ice. The Chevy slammed into a tree. His mother and his father in the front seat dead—though his mother had lived long enough that he could remember the sound of her, groaning, while the men worked to get her out, the body of his father, dead across the front seat of the car, his head in her lap. Frank, in the back—his only injury a broken wrist—had seen it all.

There had been a baby sister too. In those days, people just held their babies on their laps when they rode in cars. She was dead also.

We sat there for a minute, saying nothing. Maybe my mother was just reaching for her napkin, but her hand grazed Frank's and lingered there a second.

These are the best biscuits I ever had, my mother told him. Maybe you'll tell me the secret.

I'd probably tell you everything, Adele, he said. If I get to stick around long enough.

He asked if I played baseball. What he asked, actually, was which position I favored. The idea of none, unfathomable.

I played one season of Little League but I was terrible, I said. I didn't catch one ball the whole time I played left field. They were all glad when I quit.

I bet your problem was not having someone to coach you right, he said. Your mother looks to be a woman of many talents, but I'm guessing baseball may not be one of them.

My dad's big on sports, I said. He plays on a softball team.

Precisely, Frank said. Softball. What do you expect?

His new wife's kid is a pitcher, I told him. My dad works with him all the time. He used to take me out on the field with them to practice with a bucket of balls, but I was hopeless.

I think we should throw a ball around a little today, if you can fit that in your schedule, Henry, he said. You've got a glove?

Frank didn't have one for himself, but that wasn't a problem. He'd noticed there was an open area, out behind where our property ended, where a person could work on his fielding.

I thought you just had your appendix out, I said. I thought you were holding us prisoners. What happens if one of us runs away when you aren't looking?

Then you get your real punishment, Frank said. You have to go rejoin society.

What we did then: he scoped out our yard, to figure out where the chicken coop could go. Cold weather was coming, but with enough straw, chickens wintered over just fine. All they needed was a warm body to huddle up to in the night, same as the rest of us.

Frank checked out our woodpile, and when he heard the cord had just been delivered, he told my mother the guy who sold it had been shorting her.

I'd split this wood for you, but I might bust my stitches trying, he said. I bet it gets cozy here in wintertime, when the snow piles up, and you get a fire going in the woodstove.

He cleaned the filters on our furnace and changed the oil in the car. He replaced a fuse for the blinkers.

How long since the last time you rotated your tires, Adele? he asked.

She just looked at him.

While we're at it, he said, I'm betting nobody ever showed you how to fix a flat, am I right about that, Henry? One thing I'll tell you now, you don't want to wait till it happens, to learn. Particularly not if you've got some young lady in the seat beside you that you're wanting to impress. You'll be driving before you know it. That, and other things.

He did laundry. He ironed. When he washed a floor, he also waxed it. He looked through our pantry, in search of something he could make us for lunch. Soup. He'd start out with Campbell's but augment. Too bad we didn't have a patch of fresh basil growing. Next year maybe. Meanwhile, there was always dried oregano.

Then he took me out in the yard, with the new baseball he'd picked up the day before over at Price-mart.

For starters, he said, I'm just going to take a look at how you place your fingers on the stitching.

He bent over me, his long fingers over mine. This is your first problem, he said. Your grip.

We won't actually throw today, he said, after he'd shown me the good way, his way. His scar was still a little tender for that, he said. But anyway, it was a good idea for me to just get used to this feeling first. Finger the ball. Toss it lightly in the air when I walked around.

Come nighttime, he said, I'd like you to put your glove under your pillow. Breathe in the smell of the leather. Keeps you in the zone.

We were back in the kitchen now. Like some kind of pioneer woman, or a wife from an old western movie, my mother was mending Frank's pants where they'd ripped. She wanted to wash them too but then he'd have nothing to wear. He sat wrapped in a towel while she sewed, dabbing off the worst of the blood with a wet rag first.

You bite your lip when you sew, he said. Anyone ever tell you that?

Not that, or so much else he noticed about her that day. Her neck, the knuckles on her hands—no jewelry, he observed, which was a pity, she had such pretty hands. There was a scar on her knee that I'd never noticed.

How'd you get this, honey? he asked her, like it was no big deal calling her that, like it was the most natural thing in the world.

A "Stars and Stripes Forever" routine at my dancing school recital, she told him. I tapped myself right off the stage.

He kissed it.

Sometime in the late afternoon, after his pants were mended, after the soup, and the card game, and the trick he taught me—making a toothpick come out your nose—there was a knock on the door. Frank had been around long enough now, almost a day, to know this was unusual. I saw the vein in his neck flicker. My mother's eyes moved to the window: no sign of a car. Whoever it was came on foot.

You go, Henry, she said. Just let them know I'm occupied.

It was Mr. Jervis from down the street, with a bucket of late-season peaches. We've got so many of these, we don't know what to do with them all, he said. I thought your mother might find a use for them.

I took the bucket. He remained on the stoop, as if there was more to say.

Big weekend coming, he said. They say it'll get up to ninety-five by tomorrow.

Yup, I said. I saw that in the paper.

We've got the grandkids coming over Sunday. You're welcome to come by, jump in the pool, if you're around. Cool off.

They had an aboveground pool in their backyard, which sat empty most of the summer, except when the Jervises' son's family came to visit from Connecticut. A girl about my age who used an inhaler and liked to pretend she was an android, and a boy around three years old, who probably peed in the pool. I wasn't tempted.

I told him thanks.

Your mother home? he asked. It was a needless question, not only because our car was out front. Everyone on our street had to know my mother hardly ever went anywhere.

She's occupied.

You might want to let her know, in case she hasn't heard. There's some guy on the loose from Stinchfield, the state pen. They're saying on the radio he was last spotted out at the shopping plaza, coming into town. No reports of any hitchhikers or stolen cars, which means he could still be in the area. Wife's got her panties in a twist, convinced he's headed straight for our house.

My mother's sewing, I said.

I just thought I'd let your mother know. Her being on her own. You have any problems, give a jingle.

Chapter 7

After Mr. Jervis left, I went back to the kitchen. I had only been gone from the room four minutes, maybe, but even though it was my house, where I'd lived four years almost, and we'd just met Frank yesterday, I had the feeling, coming back in the room, that I was breaking something up. Like a time I walked in my father's bedroom over at our old house, and Marjorie was sitting on the bed with the baby, and her shirt was open and one of her breasts was showing, and another time when they let school out early because someone did an experiment wrong and the building filled up with sulfur smell, and there was a record playing so loud my mother didn't hear the door open and slam behind me, and from the kitchen, where I came in, I could see her in the living room, dancing. Not a regular dance with steps, or the kind she was always trying to teach me. That day she was twirling around the room like she was one of those dervishes I saw once on a National Geographic special. That's how the two of them looked, when I came back in with the peaches. Like they were the only two people in the world.

They had more than they could use, I said. The Jervises.

The other part, what Mr. Jervis said about the prison escape, I didn't mention.

I set the fruit on the table. Frank was down on his knees on the kitchen floor, fixing a pipe under the sink. My mother sat next to him, holding a wrench. They were looking at each other.

I picked a peach out of the bucket and washed it. My mother didn't believe in germs but I did. Germs are something they made up to distract people from what they should really be worried about, she said. Germs are natural. It's the things people do you have to worry about.

Good peach, I said.

Frank and my mother were still sitting there, holding the tools, not moving. Too bad they're all so ripe, she said. We'll never get through them all.

Here's what's going to happen, said Frank. His voice, which was always low and deep, suddenly seemed to drop another half octave now, so it was like Johnny Cash was in our kitchen.

We have a serious issue on our hands, he said.

I was still thinking about what Mr. Jervis said. People out looking for the escaped prisoner. From the newspaper, I knew they'd got roadblocks on the highway. Helicopters over by the dam, where someone thought they spotted a man matching the description, only now they were saying he had a scar over one eye and possibly a tattoo on his neck of a knife or a Harley, something along those lines. Now was the moment Frank was going to take out a gun, or a knife maybe, and wrap his lean, muscled arm around my mother's neck, that he'd just finished admiring, and press the knife against her skin, and guide us out to the car.

We were his ticket across state lines. That was the story. I'd watched enough episodes of *Magnum, P.I.* to get it. Only then Frank turned around to face us, and he was holding a knife.

These peaches, he said, looking even more serious than before. If we don't put them to use soon, they're goners.

What did you have in mind? my mother said. There was a sound to her voice I could not remember ever hearing. She was laughing, not the way a person does if you tell them a joke, but more how it is when they're just in a good mood and feeling happy.

I'm going to make us a peach pie, like my grandmother did it, he said.

First thing, he needed a couple of bowls. One to make the crust. One for the filling.

Frank peeled the peaches. I cut them up.

Filling is easy, Frank said. What I want to talk about is crust.

You could tell, the way he reached for his bowl, that this man had made more than a few pies in his life.

First off, you need to keep your ingredients as cool as possible, he said. Hot day like this, we have a challenge on our hands. We need to move fast, before the heat gets to them. If the phone rings when you're making crust, you don't pick it up. (Not that this was likely to be a problem at our house, where days went by sometimes that nobody called, unless it was my father, confirming plans for our weekly dinner.)

As he set out the ingredients around our work area, Frank talked about his life on the farm with his grandparents. His grandmother mostly, after his grandpa's tractor accident. She was the one who raised him from age ten on up. A tough woman, but fair. You didn't do your chores, you knew the consequences, no discussion. Clean the barn all weekend. Simple as that.

She had read out loud to him at night. *Swiss Family Robinson. Robinson Crusoe. Rikki-Tikki-Tavi. Count of Monte Cristo.* We didn't have television in those days, he said, but there was no need, the way she could read out loud. She could have been on the radio.

She had told him not to go to Vietnam. Ahead of her time, that woman understood no one was going to win that war. He thought he was going to outsmart them all. Stay in the reserves, get his G.I. bill college education. Next thing he knew he was eighteen years old, on a plane to Saigon. Got there two weeks before the start of the Tet Offensive. Of the twelve men in his platoon, seven went home in a box.

I wanted to know if he still had his dog tags. Or souvenirs. An enemy weapon, something like that.

I don't need one thing to remind me of those days, he said.

Frank had made enough pies in his life—none lately, but this was like riding a bicycle—that he didn't need to measure the flour, though just for my information he said he favored starting out with three cups of flour. That way you'd have extra crust, to make a turnover, or if there was some young whippersnapper around, you could give him the dough to cut out shapes with a cookie cutter.

He also didn't measure the salt he put in, but he figured it to be three-quarters of a teaspoon. Piecrust is a forgiving thing, Henry, he told me. You can make all kinds of mistakes, and still come out OK, but one thing a person can never do is forget the salt. It's like life: sometimes the littlest thing turns out to be the most important.

One tool he wished he had, for making this crust, was his grandmother's pastry blender. You could pick one up anyplace—we weren't speaking of fancy gourmet shops, just a regular supermarket—but his gram's had this wooden handle, painted green.

First you put the shortening in the bowl with the flour and salt. Then you cut it in, using your pastry blender, he said, though in an emergency (which was what we had on our hands, evidently) a couple of forks would do.

And about your shortening, he said. He had a few things to tell me about that. Some people use butter, for the superior flavor. Then again, nothing beats lard for contributing flakiness. This is one of the great controversies of piecrust, Henry, he said. All your life you'll meet people of the two persuasions, and you may have about as much luck convincing the one to come over to the other side as a Democrat talking to a Republican, or vice versa.

So which did he use? I asked. Lard or butter? Amazingly, we had lard in our pantry—though not real lard, as Frank would have preferred, but Crisco, from one time when my mother got it into her head to make potato chips and do some deep fat frying. We got about ten chips out of the deal, before she got tired and went to bed. Lucky for us now, the blue tin still sat on our shelf. Assuming Frank was not, as he might be, of the butter-crust persuasion.

I favor both, he said, sweeping the spatula through the glossy white Crisco and dropping a dollop in the center of the bowl with the flour. The butter was important too, however, so he sent me over to the neighbors' to borrow some. This was not the kind of thing my mother and I had ever done before. Doing this— though I was shy to ask—gave me a nice feeling, as if I was a character on some TV show from the olden days, where the characters were always dropping in on each other and doing fun things together. Like we were all normal people here.

When I came back with the butter, Frank cut up most of a stick of it into small pieces and scattered those over the flour too. No measuring with either of these ingredients, naturally, but when I asked him how much he used, he shook his head.

It's all about instinct, Henry, he said. Pay too much attention to recipes, you lose the ability to simply feel, on your nerve endings, what's needed at the time. This was also true of people who analyzed Nolan Ryan's fastball motion, or gardeners who spent all their time reading books about the best method for growing tomatoes, instead of just going out and getting dirt under their fingernails.

Your mother could probably say something about this, as it relates to the world of dancing, he said. And some other areas too, that we won't go into now.

He shot her a look then. Their eyes met. She did not look away.

One thing he would tell me, though, he said, had to do with babies. Not that he was any kind of expert, but for a brief while, long ago, he had cared for his son, and that experience more than any other had taught him the importance of following your instincts. Tuning in to the situation with all your five senses, and your body, not your brain. A baby cries in the night, and you go to pick him up. Maybe he's screaming so hard his face is the color of a radish, or he's gasping for breath, he's got himself so worked up. What are you going to do, take a book off the shelf, and read what some expert has to say?

You lay your hand against his skin and just rub his back. Blow into his ear. Press that baby up against your own skin and walk outside with him, where the night air will surround him, and moonlight fall on his face. Whistle, maybe. Dance. Hum. Pray.

Sometimes a cool breeze might be just what the doctor ordered. Sometimes a warm hand on the belly. Sometimes doing absolutely nothing is the best. You have to pay attention. Slow things way down. Tune out the rest of the world that really doesn't matter. Feel what the moment calls for.

Which—back to pie—might mean more lard than butter on some occasions. More butter than lard on others. The water, too, was a variable, depending on weather, of course. And we were speaking about ice water, naturally.

You need to use as little water as you can get away with, Frank said. Most people, when they make their crust, put in way too much. They get themselves a perfect-looking ball of dough naturally, but nobody's giving prizes for that. They're going to end up with a pasty crust. You know the kind I'm talking about. A person might as well be eating cardboard.

Here was one thing I must never forget: You could always add more water to your dough, but you could never take it out. The less water, the flakier the crust.

Mostly I was paying attention to Frank when he told me these things, and definitely, he was paying attention to me, and to the peach pie we were making.

He had this way of focusing that made it seem as if the rest of the world didn't exist.

There was something in the way he talked about the process of making a pie that commanded a person's attention, to the point where it was hard to look away even for a moment. But every now and then, as we worked, I'd look over at my mother, standing at the counter, watching us.

I might almost have thought there was this whole other person standing there, she looked so different.

She looked younger, for one thing. She was leaning against the counter, holding a peach. Now and then she'd take a bite, and when she did, because of how ripe the fruit was, the juice ran down her face, onto the flowered blouse, but when it did she didn't seem to notice. She was nodding, and smiling. She was having fun was what it looked like. I got this odd feeling, when I looked at her—and then at him. It was like some kind of electric current ran between the two of them. He was talking to me, and paying attention closely, too. But there was this other thing going on, underneath all that, not recognizable to most people, or any people for that matter. Like some kind of high-pitched frequency only certain very rare individuals could pick up. Only them.

He was talking to me. But he was sending his real message to her. And she got it.

Not that he was finished with the pie lesson: now he was telling me how you made a well in the center of the bowl and splashed in only enough ice water for the top crust first, gathering up the dough to make a ball—not a perfect round ball; that would require more water than you wanted. Let it hold together just enough so you can roll it out.

We didn't have a rolling pin, but Frank said no problem, we could use a wine bottle, with the label taken off. He showed me the motion first—swift, brisk strokes, from the center out. Then he had me try. The only way to learn anything, to do it.

Our dough, when we rolled it out on the counter, seemed hardly to hold together at all. His rolled-out dough only vaguely took the form of a circle. There were places where the pieces didn't even hold together at all, though these he pressed together with the heel of his hand.

Heel of the hand, he said. It's got the perfect texture and temperature. People buy all these fancy tools. When sometimes the best tool for the job is right there attached to your own body. Always there when you need it.

For a bottom crust, there was no big problem getting it in the pie dish. Frank and I had rolled out the dough on wax paper, and now that it was thin enough for his liking, and holding together, if just barely, he flipped the plate over, so it lay upside down over the rolled-out dough. Then he picked up the wax paper and turned the whole thing over. Peeled off the paper. Presto.

He put me in charge of the filling. He let me sprinkle the sugar on the peaches first, and a little cinnamon.

It would be great if we had Minute tapioca to soak up the juices here, he said. What do you know? We did.

My gram's secret ingredient, he said. Scatter a little of this stuff over the crust before you put your filling in—just so it looks like salt on a road in winter, when there's ice—and you've seen your last of soggy crust. This stuff soaks up the juices for you, without that cornstarch flavor. You know those pies I'm talking about here, right, Henry? The ones with that gluey consistency, like the inside of a Pop-Tart.

I did. We had about a hundred boxes of them in our freezer at that very moment.

Frank cut bits of butter over the mounded peaches in the pie dish. Then we were ready for the top crust.

This one has to stay together a little better than the bottom because we have to lift it, he told me. Still, it was always easier to add more water than take some away.

I looked over at my mother again. She was looking at Frank. He must have felt it because he looked up then himself, back at her.

Funny the way advice works, he said. A person might have been gone from your life twenty-five years. Certain things they said just stay in your head.

Never overhandle the dough. Another of his gram's sayings.

He got that one wrong, however, he told us. Thought she meant money. That was a joke, he explained. We might not have known because one thing about Frank, the muscles on his face, that pulled so tightly under the skin of his jaw, seemed never to have formed what you could call a smile.

We rolled out the top crust, also on wax paper. Only this time there was no way a person could turn the pie dish over on the dough, because there were peaches in it now. We'd have to lift that circle of dough off the sheet and flip it on top of the pie. For a split second there, our flaky crust, with only the minimum amount of ice water holding it together, would be suspended in the air. Hesitate in the act of lifting it and turning, and the whole thing would fall apart. Flip too fast, and you could miss your mark.

A person needed a steady hand, but also, a steady heart. This is a moment about faith and commitment, Frank said.

Up until now, Frank and I had worked alone, just the two of us. My mother had only been watching. Now he put a hand on her shoulder.

He said, I think you can handle this, Adele.

Some time back—I could no longer remember when this wasn't true—my mother's hands had begun to tremble. Picking up a coin from the counter, or chopping vegetables—on the rare occasions, like today, when we'd have some kind of fresh produce to cut up—her hand would sometimes shake so violently on the knife, she'd set down whatever it was she'd been cutting up and say, Soup sounds good tonight. What do you think, Henry?

Times she wore lipstick—rare times we went out—the outlines didn't always match her lips exactly right. It was the reason she'd mostly given up her cello, probably. On the frets, she had a natural vibrato, but she couldn't keep her hand steady on the bow. Something like what she'd attempted that afternoon—stitching his pants—was also a challenge. Threading a needle, impossible. I did that part.

Now my mother stepped up alongside the counter, next to where Frank had been standing with the wine bottle that had served as our rolling pin.

I'll try, she said, taking the circle of dough between the fingers of her two hands, and folding it over the way Frank showed her. He was standing very close. She held her breath. The circle of dough landed just where it was supposed to, on top of the peaches.

Perfect, honey, he said.

Then he showed me how to pinch along the sides, to fix the top crust to the bottom one. He showed me how to brush the top with milk, and sprinkle sugar on, and pierce the dough with a fork in three places, to let the steam out. He slipped the pie into the oven.

Forty-five minutes from now, we'll have ourselves a pie, he said. My grandma had a saying: even the richest man in America isn't eating tastier pie than we are tonight. That will be so for us.

I asked him then where his grandma was now.

Passed on, he said. His voice as he said this suggested it might not be a good thing, asking more.

Chapter 8

That summer, my body had been changing. The fact that I'd grown taller wasn't the main thing. My voice was deeper now, though stuck in an undependable middle range where I never was sure, when I opened my mouth to speak, whether the words that came out would be in the old high register or my new lower one. My shoulders were as thin as ever, but my neck might have filled out a little, and hair had started to grow under my arms, and lower down too, in the place I had no words for.

Here too I had changed. I had seen my father naked, and the sight had made me ashamed of my own body. Peewee, he called me, laughing. But Richard was younger than me, and I'd seen him in the shower too, and the sight had confirmed what I had already guessed. There was something wrong with me. I was a boy raised by a woman. I was a boy raised by a woman who believed this about men: Men were selfish. Men were unfaithful, and untrustworthy, and cruel. Sooner or later a man would break your heart. Where did that leave me, my mother's only child, a boy?

Sometime in the spring, it had happened for the first time: the stiffening in my groin, my private parts—this was my mother's term—pressing against the fabric of my pants at odd moments in the day, in ways I had no power to control. Rachel McCann would go up to the chalkboard to work out a math problem, and her skirt would rise up over her thigh, or I'd catch a glimpse of the crotch of Sharon Sunderland's underpants, when she was sitting on the bleachers above me at assembly, or I'd see someone's bra strap, or just the fastener of some girl's brassiere showing through the fabric of her shirt, from my seat in the desk behind hers, or my social studies teacher, Ms. Evenrud, would bend over my desk to look over how I'd formatted my bibliography, and there it was again, like a whole new body part that had come to life in my pants, where only a useless nubbin had existed before then.

I could have been happy or proud, but this was merely a new source of embarrassment. What if people saw? Walking down the halls at school now, I lived in fear of pretty girls, girls with round bottoms, girls who smelled nice, girls with breasts. I had read an article one time about a method of catching bank robbers, where the dollar bills were treated with a chemical that got activated when the money was taken out of the bag, so some kind of pressurized canister released a blast of blue paint that wouldn't wash off, on the faces of the robbers. This was how I felt about my erections—the undisguisable proof of my miserable half manhood.

There was more. The worst was not even what happened in my body, but what went on now in my brain. I had dreams every night, about women. I was so unsure how sex worked, it was hard forming pictures of things people might do, things I might do, though I knew there was a place on a woman's body where my newly sprouted organ could thrust itself in, like a drunk crashing a party. The idea of anyone ever wanting me there had not occurred to me, and because of that, every scene I invented was filled with shame and guilt.

Some of the dreams came back over and over: images of girls at my school—but never, maddeningly, the cheerleading squad. The girls who populated my dreams, uninvited, were the other type of girls, the ones who looked as uncomfortable in their bodies as I did in mine—girls like Tamara Fisher, who had grown fat in fifth grade, around the time her mother died, and now, in addition to her stomach and her wide white thighs, carried in front of her a shelf of heavy breasts that looked as though they should go on some old woman, not a thirteen-year-old. Even so, I wanted to see them. I pictured myself wandering into the girls' locker room by accident and catching sight of a huddle of girls changing there, or opening the door to a bathroom cubicle and seeing Lindsay Bruce squatting over the toilet, her pants gathered around her ankles, patting the secret place between her legs. The characters in my dreams were seldom glamorous or seductive so much as they were pathetic. Nobody more so than myself.

One recurrent dream featured me, running around a pole in a field somewhere, or maybe it was a tree. I was chasing Rachel McCann, and she was naked. As fast as I ran, I could never catch up with her, and we kept running in circles. I could see her bottom, and the backs of her legs, but never the front of her, never her breasts (small, but interesting to me now) or what lay below, in the nameless place I thought about all the time.

In this dream, an idea came to me, or you might say it came to the character that was me in my dream.

I stopped running suddenly and turned around to face the opposite direction. This way, Rachel McCann would be coming straight toward me. Finally, I'd get to see the front of her. Even dreaming, I registered how smart I was to think of this. What a good idea it had been.

Only I never got to see her. Every time I got to this part in the dream, I woke up, usually in a bed wet with my own embarrassing secretions, that I concealed from my mother by turning the sheets over, or stuffing them in the bottom of the laundry, or dabbing them with water and laying a towel on the spot until it dried.

I figured out, finally, why it was Rachel never came around the other side to face me in her nakedness. My brain could not have supplied the necessary images. Breasts I knew, though only (except for that one time, with Marjorie) from pictures. But the other—a blank.

As much time as I now spent thinking about girls, I had never spoken to a single girl at my school, except to say, Could you pass the paper back? I had no sister, no cousins. I liked the girl on *Happy Days*, and one of the *Charlie's Angels*—not the two most people considered the most beautiful, but the one with the brown hair, who went by the name of Jill on the show. I also liked Olivia Newton-John, and one particular Playmate of the Month named Kerri from an old issue of *Playboy* I found at my father's house one time and sneaked home in my backpack, though—maddeningly—the actual centerfold had been ripped out. But the only female person in my life I actually knew was my mother. In the end, whatever ideas I might have about how women were came back to her.

I knew people considered my mother pretty, even beautiful. The time she'd come to my school to see me in the play, a boy I didn't even know—an eighth grader—had stopped me on the playground and said, Your mom's hot. I was just feeling proud when he said the next part.

I bet when you grow up all your friends will want to ball her.

The fact that she was good-looking, with her dancer's shape, was only part of the story. I think my mother also gave off a kind of feeling, as strong as if she had a smell, or a sign on the front of her shirt, that told people there was no man around for her. There were other kids with divorced parents at my school, but nobody else like my mother, a person who seemed to have taken herself out of the game, like a woman from some foreign culture or a tribe in Africa I probably heard about one time, or maybe India, where once your original husband dies, or leaves, your own life is over.

In all the years since my father left, she only went on a date one time that I knew of. This was with a man who fixed our oil burner. He had been over all morning, down in our basement, cleaning the heating ducts. After, when he came up to give my mother the bill, he apologized for all the dust his work must have spread around our house.

I guess you're single, he said. No ring.

I was in the kitchen doing my homework when he said this, but he didn't seem to mind that I was there.

It can get pretty lonesome, he said. Winter especially.

I have my son, she said. She asked if he had children.

I always wanted to, he said. Then my wife left me. Now she's having someone else's kid.

I remember thinking, when he said this, how odd that sounded. It seemed like who a person had would be their own child, not anybody else's. I was my mother's, but now I was wondering: Did the baby Marjorie had belong to my father?

You like dancing? he asked her. Because there's a function coming up at the Moose Lodge this Saturday. If you aren't busy.

Did she like dancing? There was the question. My mother couldn't lie.

He brought flowers when he came to pick her up. She wore one of her dancing skirts that swirled out when she turned, not like how she had dressed that time long ago, when she met my father, and her underwear showed, but this time just enough to accentuate the moves and show off her legs.

Her date had also dressed up. When we'd met him, he'd been wearing his heating company uniform, with his name—Keith—over the left side of his chest, but tonight he was wearing a shirt made out of some kind of synthetic fabric that stuck to his body, which was very thin, and this shirt had been unbuttoned enough that you could see a little chest hair, which gave the impression that he'd thought about how this would look and possibly even arranged the hair to stick out at the top. Because I had seen my mother getting ready, and how she'd changed her outfit three times before deciding on this one, and standing in front of the mirror arranging her hair, now I pictured him, fluffing that chest hair so it stuck out the top of the shirt.

I had no chest hair. My father had a lot of it, but nothing about me resembled him. Sometimes I wondered if maybe I wasn't even his real son, and if maybe his real kid had always been Richard. That I was just some kind of mistake.

She did not hire babysitters, my mother. She didn't know any, considering the fact that she'd almost never gone anyplace I didn't accompany her. And anyway, she said, leaving me alone with a sitter was more dangerous than just leaving me alone. There were all kinds of people around who might seem like nice people but how could you be sure?

I set out a snack, she said. She had also left me an issue of *National Geographic* about life in ancient Greece, and a book on tape she'd sent away for about a boy who'd been shipwrecked on an island in the South Pacific where he lived on his own for three years until someone on a passing freighter had rescued him, and a project she thought I might enjoy, which was putting her penny collection into wrappers, with the promise that when we turned them in at the bank (we meaning me; she'd be out in the car) I'd get 10 percent, meaning maybe thirty-five cents if I was lucky.

You look like a princess, Keith told her. I know this will sound stupid, he said, but I don't actually know your first name. On your records down at the office we just have your last name and your account number.

He looked young, Keith. I was too young myself for the difference to seem that dramatic, between twenty-five and thirty-five, but he might not even have been twenty-five. Seeing my binder that I had out on the table again, he said, Oh, you go to Pheasant Ridge. That's where I graduated. He named a teacher he had, like I might know her.

Less than an hour after the two of them took off for the dance, my mother was home. If Keith walked her to the door, I didn't see. He didn't come in.

You can tell a lot about someone from how they dance, she said. This was a person with no sense of rhythm.

His idea of a slow dance, she said, was rocking back and forth in one spot on the floor, rubbing his hand up and down her back. Also, he smelled like furnaces. And in spite of how clear she made it, that she wasn't interested, he had still tried to kiss her before she got out of the car.

I didn't think this was my type of thing, but I thought it was only fair to give it a try, she said. Now I know, I have no interest in dating.

What interested my mother was romance. The kind of person for my mother—if such a person existed— would be unlikely to show up at the Loyal Order of the Moose.

This being Labor Day weekend, Frank said he thought we should barbecue. The problem was, we had no meat in the freezer besides Meal in Minutes dinners and Cap'n Andy fish.

I want to buy you dinner, he said. Only I've got this cash flow problem.

We had a lot of ten-dollar bills in the Ritz crackers box my mother kept on top of the refrigerator, from my last run to the bank. She took down three of them. It was unusual for my mother to take the car out more than once every few weeks, but now she said we could drive to the store.

I guess you would want to come along, she told Frank. To make sure we don't try a getaway.

Nobody laughed when she said this. Part of the odd, slightly uncomfortable feeling I had with the situation here was the way I could never be 100 percent sure who Frank was to us. He seemed like a guest we had invited over, like company that comes from out of town, but there was this other part, too, that all three of us knew, which was how he came to be with us in the first place.

That morning, when she'd come down in her flowered blouse, with her hair all fluffy, he had told her—after setting the coffee at her place, and the biscuits—not to try anything funny here.

I don't want to have to do anything we'd both regret, he said. You know what I'm talking about, Adele.

His words sounded almost like something from an old movie, a western, like what you'd see on TV on a Sunday afternoon. Still, my mother had nodded then, lowered her eyes to the table, like a kid at my school when the teacher tells them to get rid of their gum.

After he'd made the pie, he had slipped the paring knife in his pocket. Our sharpest one. The silk scarves were still out, draped over a dishtowel next to the sink. He hadn't tied her up again since that first time, but now he gestured with his head in their direction, as if no further explanation was necessary, which it wasn't, evidently, for the two of them. Only for me.

I lived here. She was my mother. Still I felt like an interloper. Something was happening here that I wasn't sure I should be seeing.

He drove. She sat next to him. I sat in the backseat, that we'd never used as long as I could remember. This is how it is in a regular family, I thought. The mom, the dad, the kid. This was how my father liked to think we were, when he and Marjorie and his new kids came to pick me up, except on those nights all I wanted was to have it be over, where now having it be over was what I dreaded. I could only see the back of her head, but I knew if I could see my mother's face, she'd have that expression I was so unfamiliar with. Like she was happy.

As we headed into town, nobody referred to the fact that the police were looking for Frank, but I was nervous. He was wearing his baseball cap, and it seemed to me he'd taken the extra precaution of pushing the brim lower than normal over his forehead. But I also knew that his main disguise was just having us with him. Nobody on the lookout for Frank was expecting a woman and a kid to be with him. And anyway, he would stay in the car. His limp was still pretty noticeable.

When we got to the supermarket parking lot, my mother handed me the bills. Frank ran over the list of things he needed: ground beef, chips, ice cream for the pie. An onion and some potatoes, for soup, Frank said.

I need a razor, he said. He preferred a straight razor, but no way were they going to carry those at Safeway.

The picture came to me again: Frank with his arm around my mother's neck, pressing a blade against her cheek. A razor now. A single bright red drop of blood dripping down her face. Her voice saying, Do what he tells you, Henry.

And shaving cream, he said. I want to clean myself up for you two. I don't want to look like a bum.

Or an escaped convict. Only nobody said that.

In the store, everyone was stocking up for the holiday weekend. For once, I was the person with only a few items, instead of how it usually went when I came here—my cart piled high with frozen dinners and soup cans, the checkout girl's comment: You expecting a hurricane or a nuclear attack?

In the line, the woman ahead of me was talking with her friend about the heat wave. Now they were saying it was going to reach a hundred on Sunday. Good time to hit the beach, but the traffic would be hell.

Finished your back-to-school shopping yet, Janice? the friend said.

Don't remind me, the first woman told her. Three pairs of blue jeans for the boys and a couple of skirts and underwear, and the bill came to ninety-seven dollars.

The cashier had gone to the city the week before. Her husband took her to see *Cats*. You know the truth? she said. For the money those tickets cost, we could stay home and watch TV and get ourselves an air conditioner.

The man behind me had spent the day cooking the tomatoes from his garden. Now he was picking up canning jars. There was a woman with a baby, who said she intended to spend the weekend sitting in her children's kiddie pool.

You hear about the guy they're looking for that jumped out the window at the prison? the back-to-school shopper asked her friend. I can't get his face out of my head.

He's probably halfway to California by now.

They'll get him eventually, the first one said. They always do.

The worst part is knowing a person like that has nothing to lose anymore, the other woman said. They're going to do anything. Life, to a person like that, is worth about ten cents.

Her friend had more to offer, but I missed it. I had reached the front of the line now, paid my money, ran out with the groceries. For just a moment, I couldn't find our car, then I spotted them. Frank had driven around the side of the building, where the Home Depot was. They had one of those swings made of cedar logs set up in the front, an end-of-season sale. The two of them were sitting in it, and he had his arm around her. The car was turned off, but with the key in the accessory position so the radio could still play, and the song was "Lady in Red."

They didn't notice I was back. I pointed out that we should get on home before the ice cream melted.

It wasn't all that late when we finished the pie, but I told them I was tired. I went up to my room and put on the fan. It was nine o'clock, but still hot enough that I took off all my clothes except my boxers, and put a single sheet over myself.

I had my issue of *Mad* magazine, but I had a hard time concentrating. I was thinking about the photograph of Frank on the front page of the newspaper that morning, and how the paper had sat there all day without one of us opening it to read the whole story. I knew from the headline there was a search going on, and that he'd killed someone, just not the particulars. In a funny way, it seemed rude to read about it, with him right there.

Downstairs, I could hear the murmur of their voices, and the sound of running water as they cleaned up, but not the words they were saying, and this would have been true even if the fan was not on high. Later, the voices said less, but there was music—an album my mother loved, Frank Sinatra singing ballads. Good dancing music, if a person knew what they were doing.

At some point I must have fallen asleep, because I was sleeping when I heard the sound of feet on the stairs. The night before, he had stayed on our couch, but this time, along with the familiar sound of my mother coming up, there was another footstep, heavier, and his low voice, that seemed to come from another whole place, somewhere deep and dark and still, like a cave or a swamp.

Still no words, just their two voices, and the hum of the fan, and from outside the open window, the sound of crickets, and a car on the road, though never as far as our driveway. Someone—probably Mr. Jervis—had a ball game on, that he must be listening to out in his yard because it was cooler there. Now and then I heard the sound of cheering and knew the Red Sox must have done something good.

Someone had run the shower, and the water had kept running for a long time, longer than any shower I ever took, so long for a moment I wondered if something had happened and I should get up and check to make sure we didn't have a broken pipe, but another part of me knew not to. Moonlight was coming in the window now. Her bedroom door creaked open. Organ music from the ball game on the radio. The voices again. Whispering now. The only words I could make out: *I shaved for you.*

The place where my head lay, against the thin wall of my tiny room, backed up against the headboard of her bed, on the other side. Over the years, I would sometimes hear her voice as she slept—the kind of murmur a person makes in the middle of a dream. I must have been familiar with the sound her bedsprings made, or the winding of her alarm clock, and afterward, the ticking, but I had never thought about those things any more than I thought about the sound of my own heart beating. My room was close enough to hers that I could hear all these things, hear the sigh she sometimes made drawing back the sheets, the sound of her water glass when she set it on the table, or the creak of the window when she opened it to get a breeze, as she did now. Hot night.

She must have heard the sounds from my room too, though this had never occurred to me before. Now I thought about the nights, recently, when I'd moved my hand over my unfamiliar new body, my breath becoming rapid, the short, low whoosh of air that escaped from my lips when it was over. Only now did I think about it, because now there was a voice on the other side of the wall, murmuring, and hers murmuring back. No longer even words. Sounds and breath, bodies moving, the slap of the headboard against wallboard, and then a single long cry, like a bird in the night who had spotted its mate, or a nesting loon when an eagle flies overhead. Distress call.

On the other side of the wall, hearing this, I felt my body stiffen. I lay that way for many minutes—ball game over now, voices in the next room stilled, with no sound but the whirring of the fan—until at last, not soon enough, I fell asleep.

Chapter 9

Saturday. What woke me was the sound of knocking on our door. I knew, from the smell of the coffee again, that Frank must be downstairs, but he couldn't answer it, and I figured my mother would still be asleep. I ran downstairs in my pajamas and opened the door. Not all the way, just partly.

My mother's friend from before, Evelyn, was standing on the front step—the first time she'd come to our house in almost a year, probably. The oversize stroller with Barry in it was a few inches below, on the cement walk leading up to the door. One look at Evelyn and you knew, she was in rough shape—that crazy perm of hers shooting out in all directions and her eyes sort of bloodshot. I knew, from all the hours I used to hear her talking to my mother, those times she came over, that Evelyn only slept a few hours every night.

I'll tell you one thing, Adele, she used to say. Life's no day at the beach.

I need to talk to your mom, she said. No need to ask if she was home. Even though we hadn't seen her for months, Evelyn knew how it was here.

She's sleeping. I had stepped outside, rather than invite her in, knowing Frank was there in the kitchen. Making French toast or something, from the smell of the butter on the pan.

I just got a call from my sister in Mass, she said. Our father had a stroke. I need to get down there.

This wouldn't be a trip for Barry, she said. I was hoping your mother could look after him for the day. Both my regular sitters went away for the long weekend.

I looked behind her, toward her son. It had been a while since I'd seen him. He was bigger than I remembered, with a faint down of hair on his lip now. He was waving his arms, as if bugs were swarming around him, though they weren't.

I packed a lunch for him, she said. His favorite foods. He's had his breakfast and diaper change. Your mother wouldn't have to do much. I could be back by dinnertime if I take off now.

Inside the house, I could hear the radio again, that classical station Frank favored. From the top of the stairs, my mother was calling down, Who is it? Then she was in the doorway too, still in her bathrobe. Her face had a softness to it. There was a mark on her neck. I wondered if he'd put one of the scarves on her again, too tight, but from the looks of her, she was OK. Just different.

It's not the best timing, Evelyn, my mother said.

They're not expecting my dad to hold on long, Evelyn told her.

Normally I wouldn't think twice, my mother said. It's just not a very good time right now.

My mother looked in the direction of the kitchen as she spoke. The smell of coffee. The sound of Frank, whistling.

I wouldn't ask if I had other options, Evelyn said. You're my one hope.

I want to help you, my mother said. It's just hard.

I promise he'll be good, Evelyn said.

Evelyn was smoothing down Barry's hair as she talked. Remember Henry and his mom, Barry? And all the good times you two used to have?

OK, said my mother. I guess we could handle this. For a little while.

I owe you, Adele. Evelyn tipped the front two wheels on the stroller up onto the stoop, so for a second, Barry's head seemed to be almost upside down.

He made a noise a little like the ones I'd heard on the other side of the wall the night before. Just sounds, but maybe they were joyful. Hard to say.

Hey, Barry, I said. How's it going?

I owe you, Adele, Evelyn said again. Anytime I can take Henry for you. (Like I was the equivalent of Barry. Like I'd ever want to spend a day at their house.)

I know you're in a rush, Evelyn, my mother said. So don't worry about anything else. We can get Barry's chair inside. Henry's really strong now.

I should get myself to the highway, Evelyn told her. The earlier I get on the road, the sooner I can get back. Put his chair in front of the TV and he'll be happy. He loves cartoons. And then there's the telethon. Jerry Lewis.

Don't worry, my mother said. We'll take him from here.

Back in the days when Evelyn and her son used to come over more, my mother used to say we needed to make our house handicap accessible, but then they stopped coming by and we never did. Now we had to lift Barry's special hi-tech chair up the steps and into the living room.

The chair, with Barry in it, was heavier than we expected. After Evelyn drove away, Frank came out from the kitchen. He lifted the chair right up off the ground and carried it into the house, but gently. He took care, when they got to the living room, that Barry didn't hit his head on the sides of the door. After Frank set him down, he adjusted Barry's head, which had flopped over to one side in transit.

Here you go, buddy, he said.

I turned on the set.

Through the passageway, into the kitchen, I saw Frank and my mother. His hand reaching to open a cupboard over the stove, brushing across her neck, as if by accident.

She looked at him.

Sleep well?

She just looked at him. You know the answer.

It was Frank who fed Barry his breakfast. Evelyn had told us he'd eaten already, but when he saw the French toast, he got excited, so Frank cut a couple of slices into small pieces for him. For the second time in a day and a half, he was feeding someone here, but with Barry it was different. When Frank had placed the spoon between my mother's lips, the sight had seemed so intimate I had to look away.

After the meal was over, Frank carried Barry into the living room and set him and his chair in front of the television. His mother had put a windbreaker on him, and a cap, but we took these off. Already, though it wasn't even seven thirty yet, the air was heavy with moisture and heat.

You know what I think you could use, buddy? Frank said. A nice cool sponge bath.

He had gotten a bowl out of the cupboard then and filled it with ice cubes and a little water. He brought the bowl in the living room, along with a hand towel, that he dipped in the cold water before wringing it out.

He unbuttoned Barry's shirt and drew the cloth over his smooth, hairless chest, his neck, his bony, birdlike shoulders. He drew the cloth over Barry's face. The sound Barry made suggested he was happy. His head, that so often seemed to roll around with no particular pattern or connection to the rest of him, seemed more steady than usual, his eyes fixed on Frank's face.

It's got to feel hot in that chair, huh, buddy? Frank said. Maybe this afternoon I'll carry you up to the tub, give you a real bath.

More noises from Barry. Joy.

On the front page of the paper, another story about record temperatures, anticipated traffic jams on the highway to the beach, danger of blackouts from over-use of air conditioners. But all we had was a fan.

I want to take a look at your leg, my mother said to Frank. Let's see how it's healing.

He rolled his pants leg up. The blood had dried along the cut place. In other circumstances, this would have been an injury that warranted stitches, but we all knew that wasn't an option here.

The place on his head where the glass had slashed into his skin no longer looked alarming either. If it wasn't for the place in his belly where they'd cut out his appendix, Frank said, he'd be splitting that wood for us. There was a satisfaction to be had in splitting wood, he said. Get all your anger out, in a way that didn't hurt anyone.

What anger is that? I asked. I didn't want it to be about me, something I'd done. I wanted him to like me, stay around. I already knew he liked my mother.

Oh, you know, he said. Late-season Red Sox. Every year, around this time, they start screwing up.

I didn't think that was really it, but I didn't say anything either.

Speaking of baseball, he said. Where's that glove of yours? After I help your mother with a few chores, what do you say we throw around the ball a little?

Barry and I watched *Fantastic Four,* and *Scooby-Doo.* Normally my mother would never have let me watch so many cartoons, but this was a special situation.

When *Smurfs* came on, I tried changing the channel to a less babyish show, but Barry started making a squealing noise, like a puppy when you step on its paw, so I let him watch that one. The show was just finishing when Frank came back down the stairs from wherever he'd been, helping my mother, to say he was in the mood for catch, how about it?

I told him I was terrible at sports, but Frank told me not to say those words. If you act like something's too hard, it will be, he said. You got to believe it's possible.

All those years in stir, he said. I never let myself believe I couldn't get out. I just bided my time and thought positive. Looked for my opening. Made sure I'd be ready, when it came along.

None of us had brought up the topic of the escape until this. It surprised me that Frank would talk about it.

I didn't know my appendix was going to be my ticket, he said. But I was ready for that window. I'd gone through it a million times already in my head. I'd worked out all my moves—the jump, and how to land it. I would have got it right, too, if there hadn't been a stone under the grass, where I wasn't counting on one. That's what did my ankle in.

I knew I'd need a hostage, he said. A particular type of person.

He looked at my mother. My mother looked at him.

Then again, he said, it's an open question, which person is the captor here, which is the captive.

He bent his head close to her ear and brushed her hair away, as if to speak directly into her brain. Maybe he thought I wouldn't hear, or maybe he was just beyond caring.

I am your prisoner, Adele, was what he said to her.

Chapter 10

I thought we'd just leave Barry where he was, but Frank figured he'd enjoy watching, so he carried him outside and set him in a lawn chair, with the Red Sox cap on that he'd picked up for himself at Pricemart. We were far enough back from the road that no one could see us, besides Barry.

It's your job to root for your favorite team, my friend, Frank told him.

Don't get your hopes up, I told him. You never saw anyone suck at baseball worse than me. (Barry, maybe. But I didn't want to hurt his feelings.)

Want to run that by me again? Frank said. Didn't you hear anything I told you about thinking positive?

Oh right, I said. I'm going to be the greatest center fielder since Mickey Mantle.

Mantle didn't play center field, Frank said. But that's the idea.

Here was the odd thing. When Frank threw the ball, I caught it. After my mother came out, and we gave her my glove and told her to take the catcher position, I hit his pitches. Not all but more than normal. You might have thought he was just feeding me candy, but that didn't even seem to be the case.

He had stood beside me on the imaginary plate and placed my hands on the bat, repositioning the angle of my elbow and wrist, a little the way my mother did when she had taught me the fox-trot.

See the ball, he said, under his breath, just before the pitch left his hand. I got so I was saying the words too, like they would bring me a hit. It seemed they did.

If I had a whole season to work with you, he said, we could really get somewhere with your game.

A lot of your problem was in your head. You see yourself screwing up, it's going to happen.

Picture yourself jumping out a hospital window and landing on two feet—a little glass on your head maybe, a gash down one side of your shin—you're out of there.

To be honest, he said, the person whose arm worries me here isn't you, Henry. It's your mother.

LABOR DAY · 121

You could use some serious remedial work, Adele, he said. You, I might need to work with you a lot longer. Years possibly.

Seeing her laugh like that, I realized it was a sight I hadn't witnessed in a long time. I was catcher now. Frank was still pitching, but now he stepped away from the spot he'd designated as the mound and approached my mother on the plate. He positioned himself so he could wrap his long arms around her. Send one our way, Henry, he said, tossing me the ball.

Only one pitch, since there was no catcher. I raised my arm and released the ball. The two of them swung. There was a hard, solid cracking sound. The ball went flying.

From over in his lawn chair, Barry let out a yelp.

My father called. He and Marjorie and the kids were at a cookout. He wanted to know if we could do our Friendly's night tomorrow instead of tonight. There was a sound to his voice, as he said this, that reminded me of how people acted on the phone, times when my mother got me to help her out with MegaMite, and I'd knock on the door of someone who used to be a customer, but didn't want to buy vitamins anymore, and I knew they were just wishing I'd go away so they could get back to their life and stop feeling guilty.

You and your mother doing OK? he said. His voice had that sound where I knew he was feeling sorry for us, at the same time he just wanted to get off the phone and back to his other family, where things were easier.

We've got friends over, I told him. As Frank would have said, I could pass a lie detector test with that statement.

Evelyn also called. Traffic had been so bad on Route 93 it had been two o'clock when she reached the hospital. They were waiting to talk with the doctor now. She was hoping Barry could stay on till after dinnertime.

Just get here when you can, Evelyn, I heard my mother say into the receiver. He seems to be doing all right.

Evelyn must have asked about the diaper situation then. That was the part that worried her. He was a big boy now, Barry. Not the easiest thing anymore, lifting him out of the chair.

My mother didn't say Frank was the one who'd changed him. Frank, the one who'd carried him back into the house after the baseball practice and run him a bath, filled it with ice cubes and shaving cream. From where I sat, in my room, I could hear the two of them: Barry making small, cooing noises; Frank whistling.

What kind of idiot am I? Frank said. I never got around to introducing myself, buddy. My name is Frank.

Barry made a sound then.

That's right, Frank told him. Frank. My grand-mother called me Frankie. Either one is fine by me.

He made us dinner again. My mother sat on the edge of the counter, sharing a beer with him. She had dug up an old Chinese fan, probably from some dance rou-tine she'd done one time. Now she was fanning him.

I bet you could think up a nice dance to do for me with that one, Adele, he told her. You'd probably have some great-looking outfit to go with it. Or not.

Nobody was hungry, due to the heat, but Frank had made a cold curry soup with the last of the peaches and the last of an old container of hot sauce we had, from some take-out food we got once. After, my mother fixed root beer floats, and Barry and I sat in the backyard, beyond the sight lines of the Jervises' aboveground pool, where we could hear the splashing of the girl with asthma and her little brother. When the bugs got bad, we came inside and turned on the television. They were showing *Close Encounters of the Third Kind.* Frank propped up Barry in his chair and wrapped another cool cloth around his neck. My mother made popcorn.

When we heard the sound of Evelyn's car pulling up, Frank slipped up the stairs, as they had planned he would. As far as Evelyn was concerned, it had been just the three of us here. Me and my mother, and her son.

She had stepped into the living room now. Her father was stabilized, she said. Still in intensive care, but no longer critical. How can I ever repay you, Adele? she said.

I knew my mother just wanted them to go, but Evelyn had been driving for two hours. You look like you could use a cold glass of water, my mother told her.

She had just come back with the water when the news came on. An update. Energy consumption during the day's heat wave had left the area in the danger zone for major power outages, and there was still the rest of a long hot holiday weekend ahead of us.

We know it's hot out there, folks, the newscaster was saying, but our friends at Public Service are asking us all to turn off those air conditioners whenever possible. If the heat's getting to you, consider a cold shower.

In other news, he said, police in the tristate area continue their search for the prisoner at large in the region since Wednesday.

The photograph of Frank flashed on. Up until this moment, Barry had seemed only marginally aware of his surroundings, but as the image of Frank filled the screen, he began to wave his arms and call out, as if greeting an old friend. He was making noises, slapping his head, slapping the television.

In the past, I knew, one of Evelyn's themes in her conversations with my mother had to do with how people were always underestimating her son's intelligence and comprehension of what was going on. For a while there, she had campaigned to get him mainstreamed into a regular classroom at school. But now, as Barry yelped and waved, she seemed barely to notice his agitation and excitement—the way he had started flailing his arms, more furiously than normal, with his shoeless feet kicking air. His eyes, that normally seemed not to focus, were locked on the television screen.

Time to get you home, son, his mother said, sounding weary.

Together, the three of us—Evelyn, my mother, and me—backed the wheelchair through the open door of our house—out into the darkness—and lowered it onto the walk. We watched as Barry's mother slid the chair onto the ramp and up into the back of her van and buckled him into place. As the rear doors closed, I could see his face. He was still calling out, the same one syllable, the first word I had ever heard him utter that I understood.

Over and over, he was saying it, garbled but intelligible. *Frank.*

That night again, I heard them. They had to have known the sound would carry through the wall between our rooms. It was as if they didn't care anymore who knew or what anybody thought about it, including me. They were in their own place now, and it was like a whole other country, a whole other planet.

It went on for a long time, their lovemaking. Back then I didn't use that word for it—not that word or any other. It was nothing I'd known in my own experience or anyone else's either. Nothing I encountered on those rare times I slept at my father's house, though he shared a bed with Marjorie. Nothing I could imagine happening, in any of the other houses on our street, and nothing like any scenes they showed on television either—those times Magnum P.I. leaned in to kiss that week's beautiful woman, or some pair of guest stars nuzzled in the moonlight on *The Love Boat*.

The way I imagined what went on between my mother and Frank on the other side of the wall, though I tried not to, they were like two people shipwrecked on an island so far away from anyplace no one would ever find them, with nothing to hold on to but each other's skin, each other's bodies. Maybe not even an island, just a life raft in the middle of the ocean, and even that was falling apart.

Sometimes the headboard banged against the wall for whole minutes at a time, as regular and steady as the sound of Joe's wheel in his cage, the endless circles he made. Other times—and these were harder to lie there and listen to—the sounds were like what you might expect to come from a nest of baby animals. Bird sounds, or kittens. And a low, slow, satisfied growling, like a dog on the floor by the fire with a bone, working it over in his mouth, licking it clean to get the last piece of anything that tasted of meat.

Now and then, a human voice. *Adele. Adele. Adele. Frank.*

They never, that I heard, spoke about love, as if they were past even that.

These moments, I knew, they were not thinking about me lying in my bed on the other side of the wall, with my Einstein poster and my mineral collection and my Narnia books and my signed letter from the *Apollo 12* astronauts and my *Thousand and One Great Party Jokes* and the note I'd saved from the one time Samantha Whitmore ever acknowledged my existence on the planet: Do you have tomorrow's math homework?

These moments, they were not thinking about the heat wave, or conserving electricity, or the Red Sox, or peach pie, or back-to-school shopping, or his appendix stitches, though I had seen them and knew they were still raw on his lower belly, same as the place was, along his calf muscle, where the glass had cut him. They were not thinking about third-floor windows or TV anchor-people or police roadblocks or the helicopters we had heard circling town all afternoon the day before. What were they expecting to see—a trail of dripping blood? People tied to trees? A campfire, and a man beside it roasting squirrel meat?

So long as we stayed inside this house, no one would know he was here. Not in the daytime, maybe, but at night anyway, nobody could get to us. We were like three people not so much inhabiting Earth as orbiting above it.

Not that either, exactly. The configuration was two and one. They were like the two *Apollo* astronauts who moved together along the surface of the moon, while their trusty companion stayed behind in the space capsule, monitoring the controls and making sure things were all right. Somewhere far below, the citizens of Earth awaited their return. But for the moment, time was suspended, and not even atmosphere existed.

Chapter 11

Then morning came—Sunday now—and we had to deal with things again. Sometime that afternoon my father would be coming by to get me, and though I didn't want to go with him any more than he wanted to take me, I would.

School was due to start on Wednesday—seventh grade. Nothing to look forward to there but more of where I'd left off in the sixth, only the boys who called out *faggot* and *asshole* under their breath when I walked past in the halls would be that much bigger now, while I—in spite of what my mother claimed the MegaMite had done for me—looked small as ever.

The girls' breasts might have grown over the summer—probably would have—but all that would mean was more trouble, concealing their effect on me, every time I got up from my desk to change classes. Who wouldn't know my terrible secret, watching the way I carried my books, crotch level, making my way from social studies to English, English to science, science to lunch? Never mind that no one cared, my useless boner would tirelessly announce itself, like the way Alison Smoat kept raising her hand with some comment in social studies, though the teacher never called on her. Knowing—as we all had by then—that once she started talking, you could never shut that girl up.

There would be basketball tryouts. Then the election of class officers. They'd cast the fall musical. The different groups of students who mattered in this place would claim their tables in the lunchroom, making it clear to the rest of us all the places we shouldn't even think of sitting. The principal would give his talk about peer pressure and drugs; the health teacher, after reminding us we were too young for sexual activity, would show us what a condom looked like and roll it out over a banana, as if I'd have any use for one, anytime in the next decade, or ever, maybe.

Visualize what you want to happen, Frank had said to me, from his improvised pitcher's mound. But I did my visualizing mostly in my bed.

I visualized Rachel McCann taking off her bra for me then. See how they grew over the summer? she said. Would you like to touch them?

I visualized some girl I couldn't even identify coming up from behind while I was working on my locker combination, putting her hand over my eyes, whirling me around and sticking her tongue in my mouth. I couldn't see her face, but I could feel her breasts pressing against me, and her tongue on my teeth.

Why don't you drive for a change, Henry? my mother says. What do you say we head out to the beach?

Only it's not my mother and me. It's the three of us, her in the back, me at the wheel, Frank on the seat beside me, just to make sure I'm doing it right, the way a father would, but not mine.

What do you say we get out of town for a while? Frank says. Head north. Try someplace different.

We set Joe's cage on the seat next to my mother, and a few books maybe, a pack of cards, my mother's tape of sad Irish folk songs and a few of her outfits no doubt. No foodstuffs. We'll stop at restaurants when we get hungry. I will bring my comic book collection but no puzzle books. I only liked those puzzles so much, I realize now, because there was so little else to do, but now there is.

It surprises me that this is so, but I may even throw the baseball and my glove in the trunk. In the past, I always approached my father's suggestion that we play catch with a sense of anxiety and dread, but with Frank it had felt good to throw around the ball that way. With him, I wasn't ridiculous.

We drive north, into Maine, the radio playing. At a shacky little place on the water—Old Orchard Beach—we stop for lobster rolls, and my mother gets fish and chips.

Boy, these taste a lot better than Cap'n Andy's, she says, putting one in Frank's mouth.

How's your lobster roll? he asks me, but my mouth is too full to answer so I just grin.

We get lemonade, and after, ice-cream cones. At the next table, a girl in a sundress—because it's summer again, or maybe Indian summer—is licking on her own cone, but lowers it now and waves. She doesn't know anything about who I was at my old school, who my mother was in our old town, or about Frank's picture in the paper.

I saw you carrying a copy of *Prince Caspian,* she says. That's my favorite book.

Then she's kissing me too, but differently from how the other girl did it. This one is long and slow, and as we kiss each other, her hand is pressing against my neck and stroking my cheek, and mine is in her hair too and then on her breast, but softly, and of course I have a hard-on now again, only this time there is nothing embarrassing about it.

Your mother and I thought we'd take a little walk on the beach, son, Frank says to me. And the thought occurs to me that here is one of the best parts about his showing up. I am not responsible for making her happy anymore. That job can be his now. This leaves me free for other things. My own life, for instance.

Coffee on the stove again. The third morning in a row, and now I was almost used to it. There was a wet place on my sheets as usual, but I was not as concerned as I used to be. My mother wasn't monitoring my laundry. She had other things on her mind.

This time, she was already up when I got downstairs. The two of them were sitting at the kitchen table, with the paper open. Some family's boat capsized at Lake Winnipesaukee the day before and now they were looking for the father's body. An old lady on a senior citizens' excursion to the outlet stores in North Conway collapsed of heatstroke on the bus and died. The Red Sox were holding on to second place, with the playoffs around the corner. The old hopes of September rising once more.

But the story my mother and Frank were reading was none of these. Maybe they read it, maybe they stopped at the headline: "Police Intensify Search for Prisoner on the Lam." The authorities were offering a $10,000 reward for information leading to the apprehension of the man who escaped from Stinchfield Penitentiary on Wednesday. Some officials were speculating that given the issues of the holiday weekend, combined with what they would guess to be the severity of the man's injuries and the fact that he was recuperating from surgery, he might still be in the vicinity, possibly holding some local citizen or citizens hostage. The prisoner might or might not be armed but was considered dangerous regardless. In the event that anyone spotted him, under no condition should he or she attempt to apprehend the man. Contact your local police authorities, the story said. The reward would be paid following a successful arrest.

I stepped into the mudroom. It had been a few days since I'd cleaned out Joe's cage. I picked him up and held him in the crook of my arm while I laid down a fresh piece of newspaper. Not the one with Frank's face on the front, though it was there in the stack. The sports section.

Normally, Joe would be doing laps on his exercise wheel this time of day. First thing in the morning he was always his friskiest. But today, he had just been lying on the floor of the cage when I came in, panting. It was the heat probably. Nobody would want to move around any more than necessary on a day like this one.

I stood there in the mudroom for a minute then, stroking his fur. He nibbled gently on my finger. Through the
screen door, the sound of my mother's voice, talking to
Frank.

I have a little money, she was telling him. After my
mom died, I sold the house. It's just sitting in my savings account.

You need your money, Adele, he said. You've got
a son to raise.

You need to go someplace safe.

Suppose you came with me?

Are you asking me?

Yes.

Over lunch that day, Frank told us how much better
the spot on his abdomen was, where they'd cut into
him. He should have asked the doctor to save him the
appendix, put it in a jar or something, he said. I'd like
to see what the little bugger looked like that made all
this possible, he said.

Getting out. Meeting you.

When he said that, I figured he meant my mother,
though we were both at the table.

He had never told us how long he'd been locked
up, or how much more time he was supposed to stay
there before they let him out. I could have read it in

the paper, but it would have felt like cheating, doing that. Same as it would asking the details of what he was in for.

They were in the kitchen, washing the dishes. My old job, but I wasn't needed for that one anymore, so I lay on the living room couch, flipping the channels and listening.

Good as it feels, he said, to wake up where I am now (this would be in my mother's bed, with her next to him), I can't call myself a free man until the day comes I can walk down the street with my arm around your waist, Adele. All I'd ever ask for out of life.

Nova Scotia, she said. Prince Edward Island. Nobody bothers you up there.

They could raise chickens. Have a garden. The Gulf Stream flowed through the ocean there.

My ex-husband would never let me take Henry away, my mother said.

You know what that means, then, don't you? he told her.

They were leaving, and they were leaving me. All this time I'd been picturing how now it would be the three of us together, like when we played catch in the yard, only really, it was going to be the two of them. And me left behind. That's what I concluded.

One day soon—not today, because the bank would be closed, and not tomorrow either, for the same reason, but after that, they would drive over to her bank. A couple of years had passed since my mother had last entered the bank, but this time she would. She would go up to the teller window herself this time—Frank would be waiting in the car—and say, I want to make a withdrawal. Ten minutes later—because it might take that long, counting out the bills—she would go back out to the car, with the sack of money in her arms, and place it on the floor of the car.

What do you say we blow this town? he'd say. Words from some old western I'd watched, from back in the day.

I'll miss him so much, my mother would say. Meaning me. Maybe she'd start to cry then, but he'd comfort her, and pretty soon she'd stop.

You can have another baby, Frank would tell her. Same as your ex-husband did. We'll raise our kid together. You and me.

And anyway, your son will be all right. He can go live with his father. And the stepmother, and those two other kids. They'll have a great time. His father will coach him on his baseball.

I didn't want it to, but the scene kept playing out in my brain. Him stroking her hair, telling my mother

I didn't really need her anymore. Her with her head on his shoulder, believing it.

He's not a kid anymore, Frank would tell my mother. I happen to know all he thinks about now is getting into some girl's pants. He's moving on. If you have any doubt, just take a look at the sheets on his bed. A boy that age, he only cares about one thing.

Rachel McCann's thighs. Sharon Sunderland's underpants. The tits on a Las Vegas showgirl.

It's about time you thought of yourself for a change, Adele, he would tell her. Enough of that husband-for-a-day idea. Frank could be her husband forever.

I made a racket, coming in the room, though sometimes I wasn't sure if that even mattered, my mother and Frank were so deep in their own world now. The one with only two people in it—her and him. But by the time I got to the refrigerator to take out the pitcher of milk for my cereal—real milk, for once, Frank's idea—they were talking about something else. He had noticed a spot next to the shower in the bathroom where the water had seeped under the linoleum, causing dry rot. He wanted to tackle that problem today. Remove the tile, and the punk wood underneath. Replace them with better.

Maybe we won't be staying around here long enough to make a difference, she said.

Still, he said. With something like that, it's always a good idea to take care of it. I don't like to leave a mess like that for someone else to take care of.

There it was, proof. They were leaving. What was supposed to happen to me then?

Chapter 12

Over breakfast, Frank had told us about the farm where he grew up, in western Massachusetts. His grandparents had run a pick-your-own operation—blueberries mostly, though in the later years they'd put in Christmas trees and, for the fall, pumpkins. From the age of seven, he was driving the tractor, rototilling between the rows, keeping the chickens fed, and taking care of the trees. They didn't come out shaped like Christmas trees, naturally. It was all about pruning.

His grandparents had a stand out front, where they sold their goods, along with things like his grandmother's jam, and pies she made, in berry time. Frank would have rather shoveled chicken shit all day, excuse his language, than work the farmstand, so after his grandpa died his grandmother had hired a girl to help out. Mandy, a local girl, a year older than Frank. Hard-luck background. Her mother had run off with some guy, and she never knew her father in the first place. At the point Frank met up with her, Mandy had dropped out of school. She was living at her sister's. Cleaning people's houses and picking up jobs when she could. The one at Chambers Farms, for instance.

He went out with her, if you could call it that, the summer after high school graduation. Mostly they drove around, listening to the radio and making out.

I was a virgin, Frank told my mother. As usual, the two of them appeared to carry on their conversations no differently with me around than they would have if I wasn't. I might as well have been invisible.

That fall he'd shipped out to 'Nam. A two-year tour of duty. Less said about that the better. The idea had been to get a college education when he got home, but by the time he got back, all he wanted was to find some quiet spot where people would just leave him alone. The night terrors hadn't gotten bad yet, but they'd started. There was no such thing anymore as a good night's sleep.

While he was gone, Mandy had written to him, three times. Once, right after he left, to say she would be thinking about him and put him in her prayers, not that he ever saw her as the praying type. Maybe she liked the idea of having a boyfriend overseas.

No word from her after that for all that year and most of the next one. Then out of the blue, near the end of his tour, a long letter on lined notebook paper, in the same round handwriting, leaning backward, with the happy faces in the dots when she made her *i*'s.

She wrote with news about people in their town. A boy they'd both known who'd reached into a hay baler and lost his arm. Another boy who'd crashed his car head-on into an oncoming station wagon a few months back, killing all three members of the family in the other vehicle. She had cut out the obituaries of several older people in their town—friends of his grandmother's, in some cases—who'd died of natural causes, and one, the man who'd delivered their milk, who had pulled his truck into the garage one day, closed the door, and turned on the engine. No note.

It was hard to say what the point of all this bad news was supposed to be, except that Vietnam wasn't so terrible after all, or maybe that every place else was just as bad. Life is short, why not go for it?

Her letter, and the one that arrived two days after, before he'd had a chance to answer the first, had an effect on him—though he was not yet twenty-one—of leaving the impression that tragedy and death would follow a person wherever he went in life. There was no such thing as escape, except maybe the kind that Mr. Kirby had accomplished when he pulled himself into the garage that day and turned on the ignition. If there had ever been a day when he thought that coming home would make things better, that day was past.

Now she wrote to say she was counting the days till his return. She'd made a calendar and taped it on the wall at her sister's house, she said. Would he like her to have her hair up or down when she came to pick him up?

He couldn't remember there ever being a moment when he'd asked her to be his girlfriend, or thought she was, but now it seemed that was what had happened, all by itself, like the way blueberry bushes catch the mold, or chickens know it's time to head back into the coop at night, without anybody shooing them in that direction. It wasn't like he had any better plan in mind, so why not?

She had been there at Fort Devens, the day he got off the plane. A little plumper than he remembered, thicker around the waist, but the good news had been, bigger on top too. He'd had a few times with girls in Saigon by now, and once, on leave, in Germany, but ever since getting those two letters from Mandy, he'd decided to wait till he got home. Hold on till it was her.

His grandmother had fixed up a place for him, in the back of her house, but with its own bathroom, and a mini refrigerator and a hot plate, so he could feel like he had his own apartment. This was where she drove him now. His grandmother was waiting. She looked a lot older than before. The television had been on when he came in the house—*Let's Make a Deal.* The sound of all the people in the audience screaming had made him want to cover his ears.

Can we turn that off, Grandma? he said. But even that didn't help. Down in the field, someone was running a mowing machine, and her wash must have gone on the spin cycle, and then there was the radio. The men in the barn were listening to a ball game. A roaring sound. He wasn't even sure if everyone else heard it too, or if the noise was only in his head.

I fixed you some lunch, Frankie, she said. I figured you'd be hungry.

Give me a little time, Gram, he told her. I just want to lie down for a bit. Take a shower or something.

That was what he meant actually, but when they got to the room she'd set up for him—Mandy still holding on to his uniform, like the women on *Let's Make a Deal* hanging on Monty Hall—she had locked the door behind them right away and pulled the blinds down.

Finally we get to do it, she said.

He wanted to tell her he was tired. He'd probably be more in the mood tomorrow, or even possibly a little later. But she was unbuttoning his jacket already. Then she was down on the floor, unlacing his boots. She had unbuttoned her shirt and unfastened her bra, which turned out to be the kind that opened in the front, so now her breasts tumbled out, bigger than he remembered, her nipples large and dark.

She said, I bet you've been starved for this, right, baby? Or all you got was yellow girls? You probably forgot what it was like, American pussy?

He had worried that he might not even be able to get it up, but he did. She had seen to that.

You just lay back and enjoy, Mandy told him. I'll do the work.

It was over in five minutes, maybe less. After, she had hopped up off the bed and checked her makeup. Of all the times to get a zit, she said.

It turned out she'd brought her clothes over. Underwear, deodorant, hot rollers, shampoo, Dippity-Do, even her nail kit. That night, when she came back to the room with him again, she had asked if he wanted to do it some more but when he said he was still a little tired from the plane and all, she didn't push it.

I better warn you, she said. You were so excited this afternoon, I didn't even think about making you wear a rubber. Here's hoping it's not that time of the month. My sister got knocked up the first time she and Jay did it. Which turned out to be a blessing naturally. That baby being her niece, Jaynelle.

A couple of weeks later, she told him she'd missed her period. A couple of days after that, she told him the test came back positive. Looks like you're going to be a dad, she said. Her words, when she said this, had the air of a speech she'd practiced. In the car coming back from town maybe. She had bought a maternity top already. *Baby on Board.*

I guess you'd just been storing it all up so long, those sperms of yours were three times as powerful as regular, she said.

That was the word she'd used. Sperms.

Suddenly, as if they'd been waiting just offstage the whole time, ready for someone like Carol Merrill to wheel them out, there was all this baby gear: a Swing-o-Matic and a playpen, a changing table, a high chair, and more maternity tops, and pants with elastic waistbands, and cream for preventing stretch marks that she wanted him to apply to her belly, to make him feel more involved in the pregnancy, she told him.

She had a crib picked out from the Montgomery Ward catalog, and a stroller, and a crib mobile. She had a list of girls' names she liked. If it was a boy, they'd name him after Frank, of course. Nearly everything she owned was already moved into the room at his grandmother's—her clothes filling the closet, and all but one of the drawers, her poster of Ryan O'Neal tacked on the wall, the most handsome man in the world after him, she said. But now she was saying, maybe they could spread out a little, into the rest of the house, considering his grandmother was just one person, and old. That sewing room she had, for instance, would be perfect for the baby. They should get a TV with a bigger screen.

Only much later did this occur to him. By the time the thought entered his mind, they were married. Mandy was seven months pregnant at this point—the baby not due until sometime around Valentine's Day, though their son had ended up being born in December. Frank was standing at the bathroom mirror, shaving, with all those toiletries she used lined up on the sink and on the shelf over the toilet. He was thinking about how many products women seemed to require—not his grandmother of course, but Mandy, definitely—before they could go out in the world. All the equipment that Mandy had brought over that first day he got home— her toiletries and makeup and hair care products, her creams and sprays, her eyelash curler and the bleach she used on her upper lip, the Nair for her legs, the panty liners and feminine hygiene deodorant.

One thing she'd never had with her. He had learned this when her sister was over visiting, and she got up off the couch and said, Oops, my little friend just came to visit. You got a pad, Mandy?

In all the supplies she'd laid in, back before she took the test, there had been no sanitary napkins, no tampons. As if she knew all along she wasn't going to need them for a while.

My mother and Frank were sitting in the kitchen while he told her the story of his marriage. I sat at the table too, working on my puzzle book. At one point in the story—when Frank mentioned the part about American pussy—my mother had looked over at me, as if she suddenly remembered she had a son, but I was bent over a puzzle at the time, chewing on my pencil as if everything I cared about in life was on that page. Either she figured I wasn't listening or she didn't think I understood, or possibly she knew I did but didn't care. And it was true, long before that day Frank came home from Pricemart with us, my mother used to tell me things that other people's mothers never discussed. I knew about final disconnect notices from the phone company and PMS. I had heard the story of the man who would have raped her one time, when she was leaving her waitress job at the restaurant where she used to work in Boston before she met my father, only the cook had come out at just the right moment and stopped him, only then the cook had thought that meant she owed him something too.

These were the kinds of stories I was used to hearing. Frank's wasn't all that different. Just from the man's perspective for a change. Which accounted for why I'd never heard that phrase before, American pussy.

Excuse my French, Frank had said, when he got to that part in the story. But this seemed to be for my mother's benefit as much as mine.

Frank and his grandmother had sat outside in the waiting room, when Mandy went into the hospital. That's how they did it in those days, he said.

I feel I let you down, Frankie, his grandmother had told him that day. Things happened so fast for you when you came home. I always wanted you to go to college. Have a little time to know what you wanted before everything started happening.

It's OK, Gram, he told her. He had just turned twenty-one years old. He was married to a woman who spent her afternoons watching television and talking on the phone to her sister about the lives of the characters on *All My Children*. After that first flurry of activity following his return from Vietnam, she had lost interest in sex, though he was hoping once the baby came along this might change. She had mentioned to him recently that if his grandmother would just subdivide the property and give them some of the land, they could put a trailer on it and maybe sell off another parcel to buy an RV. What kind of future was there in Christmas trees, anyway? Did he think she wanted to spend the rest of her life with a man who came home every night with sap on his hands?

Let's face it, she said, most people would rather buy an artificial tree now anyways. Then they only pay the money once, and there's no mess with all those needles falling down and jamming up the vacuum cleaner after.

Now he sat in the waiting room, outside where his wife was giving birth to their child, and suddenly he realized that in all the months he'd been home, this was the first time he had sat down alone with his grandmother. All this time, he'd been so busy with Mandy, the baby—getting married, going shopping for things.

You never really told me what it was like over there, his grandmother said, meaning in the jungle, with his platoon. All I know is pictures on the news and *Life* magazine.

It was pretty much what you'd expect, he told her. The usual. You know. War.

Your grandpa was the same way, she said. Any time I asked what happened in the Pacific, he'd want to talk about getting a new mower blade, or the chickens.

Early in the labor, they'd given Mandy the option of a spinal, and she was happy about that. Sometime that night, a nurse had come out holding their son.

All this time, they'd been so busy talking about the crib, the stroller, the car seat, the clothes, he'd almost forgotten there was going to be a baby at the end of it all. Now they were laying the blanket in his arms, with the warm, wriggling form of Francis Junior wrapped inside. A little hand reaching up through the fabric, with long, pink fingers and nails that already looked as if they needed trimming. Even before his face, it was his son's hand Frank had seen, as if he were waving, or pleading.

He had a full head of hair—red, which was surprising—and a long body, a plastic clip still attached to the place where his navel would be, a tiny perfect penis, not yet snipped like his own, with surprisingly large and perfect balls. His ears looked like tiny shells. His eyes were open, and though the nurse said he couldn't really focus yet, from his expression it appeared that he was looking straight at Frank.

Nothing bad had happened to him yet. So far, life was perfect for their son, though from this moment on, that would begin to change.

For some reason, the sight of the baby—his pale naked, defenseless body maybe—brought to Frank's mind certain images from the last two years, villages his company had moved through, as they made their way into the jungle. Other children he didn't want to think about. Hands reaching out to him, in other circumstances.

He was aware then of a roaring sound, and a high screeching noise. The floor-polishing machine, that was all, but hearing it, Frank had cupped one hand over Francis Junior's shell ears.

Too loud, he said, and only after he spoke did he realize he was actually yelling, as if there were a gun battle going on instead of a floor waxing.

I'm sure you want to see your wife, the nurse told him. *His wife.* He had almost forgotten.

They led him into the delivery room. The nurse had taken the baby from him now, so his arms were free. He knew there was something he should be doing now—put them around her? Touch her cheek? Lay a cool cloth over her forehead? He stood there with his arms dangling, unable to move.

You did a good job, he said. He's a real baby.

Now I can finally start getting back in shape, she said.

Nursing ruins your boobs, she said. She knew from seeing what her sister looked like, after seven months of Jaynelle hanging off her. Anyway, if they used bottles, Frank could help out with the feedings, which he did. At night, when the baby cried, it was Frank who rose to heat the formula and sat with the baby in the dark, on the sofa in his gram's kitchen, holding his son and watching as his mouth worked the nipple, and after, walked him around the room, rubbing his back, waiting for the burp. Sometimes, even after that, he stayed up, walking through the rooms of the house with the baby. He liked it there, just the two of them.

Sometimes he talked to his son. If Mandy had heard the things he said to Frank Junior, she would have called him mental, but alone in the night, he could explain about bass fishing, and pruning trees, and the time, when he was fourteen or fifteen, that his grandfather had taken him out to where the pumpkins were just starting to form on the vine, and told him he could carve anything he wanted in one. With his grandpa's pocketknife he'd carved the initials of a girl he liked— Pamela Wood, her initials, along with his. He had planned to give her the pumpkin by Halloween time, but when October came, she was going steady with some guy on the basketball team.

He talked to Frank Junior in the night about getting his first car, and how you needed to be sure to check the oil, which he had forgotten, which was how he came to burn up the engine on that one, though his grandpa forgave him for that.

One night, when they'd been walking around like this for hours, he told Frank Junior about the accident. How he'd sat in the backseat of the station wagon, listening to the sound of his mother moaning, unable to do anything. He told Frank Junior about the village they'd been to—him and what was left of his platoon at that point—where this buddy of his from Tennessee who had a grenade go off next to his head had gone crazy. The woman in the hut. The little girl on the mat next to her. These were things he had never talked about before, but that night he told them to his son.

Mandy liked putting the baby in outfits and taking him for walks at the mall. They had their portrait taken at Sears, in front of a scene of a field with mountains in back. Frank with his arm on Mandy's shoulder, Mandy with Frank Junior propped in front of her, his red hair combed into a single curl. Frank was worried that the flashbulb could hurt his eyes, but Mandy had laughed at that.

You're not going to raise him to be a pansy, are you? she said. Boys need to toughen up.

Almost the moment she came home from the hospital she'd wanted to get out of the house. I'm going crazy, she said, sitting around here all the time with your grandmother, hearing her stories about the old days.

So Frank took her out to dinner—an Italian place, with wine and a candle on the table where the wax burned down in rainbow colors, covering the bottle they'd stuck it in, but the spaghetti tasted like Chef Boyardee. When he got the bill, Frank had thought about how, for this much money, he could have rustled up something really nice at home. His gram's lasagna was better.

And he worried about leaving Frank Junior with his grandmother. She'd had a stroke the year before, just a small one, but the doctor said there was a fair chance it might happen again. Suppose it did, when she was watching the baby.

So mostly Frank stayed home, nights, with Frank Junior, so Mandy could go out with her sister or her girlfriends. She had found a job now—at a Wendy's that had opened up out by the highway.

One time, when they were at the mall, a couple had walked by. The woman was pregnant, looking like she had a few months to go. The man had an arm around her shoulders. They both looked young, the age of Frank and Mandy, not that he felt young anymore. But this guy had a certain kind of good looks that red-haired men possess on occasion. Not completely unlike Ryan O'Neal, though with the beginnings of a belly forming.

When the couple came within view, Frank had seen Mandy's body stiffen, and her eyes follow the man.

You know him?

Just someone that comes into the restaurant sometimes.

Then she started bowling. Then it was bingo too. Then it was drinks with her sister, and more phone calls, and one time, when he'd come in from the barn earlier than normal, he'd heard her laughing on the phone, a sound in her voice he'd never heard when she talked to him.

One night when she was supposed to be at bowling, he'd left the baby with his grandmother and drove the truck to Moonlight Lanes. The women's league doesn't play on Tuesdays, the guy told him. You must have your nights mixed up.

He drove to the Wagon Wheel out by the highway then, and when her car wasn't in the parking lot there, he tried Harlow's. She sat in a corner booth. Some guy in a Phillies shirt with a hand on her knee.

We aren't discussing this here, he said. This is for home.

He drove back in the truck and waited, but she didn't come home that night, or the next night either. Francis Junior seemed to be fine without her was the truth, and Frank was thinking, if she would just leave him the baby, everything would be OK. Day three, sometime near suppertime, she finally pulled up in front of the house. One look at her, one look at Frank, his grandmother had said, "I'll take the baby." From upstairs, he could hear her murmuring to Francis Junior. His gram was running water in the tub.

Mandy was leaving. She had met a real man, she said. Someone to take her out of here. What kind of future did he think he was making for them here, him and his Christmas trees?

I never told you before, because I didn't want to hurt you, she said. But all those times I acted like I was having a good time in bed. I wasn't.

There was more, no need for a recap. The main thing was, she didn't love him, never had. She just felt sorry for him, off in the war and everything, knowing there would be nobody to welcome him home except for a senile old woman growing pumpkins.

Why he even pursued this next was a mystery. It wasn't something he needed to know, or anything that made a difference, concerning how he felt about his son. But something made him ask her if the baby was his.

She had laughed. If she hadn't been drinking heavily already, she might not have answered as she did, but she had thrown her head back and laughed so hard it took her a moment before she gave him the answer.

That's when he pushed her. No doubt he wanted to hurt her, but he didn't expect her to fall. Her head had hit the granite of their front step, going down. A single trickle of blood coming from her ear, nothing more. Only her neck was broken.

Not right away—because at first he had just knelt there, with her head in his hands—but after a few minutes, he realized the water was still running upstairs. The tub must be overflowing, because there was water coming through the ceiling now, through the plaster. So much water now, you would have thought a pipe had burst. Like the kind of downpours they had in the jungle sometimes, only in his house.

He took the steps two at a time. He threw open the door to the bathroom. Inside, another woman crumpled on the ground, this time his grandmother. Her heart had simply stopped beating.

And in the water, red hair plastered against pale skin, his thin legs limp and still, arms by his sides, and his face staring up with a look of wonder in his eyes—

a look as if nothing less than an aurora borealis were shining down on him—lay the body of Frank Junior.

When they first brought him in, the lawyer assigned to his case had called it a clear case of manslaughter.

Frank was responsible for Mandy's death, he told them. He never meant to kill his wife but he had. That was the fact of it, and he would take his punishment.

The part they didn't expect was the next. Her sister had come forward to say the baby wasn't his, and that when Frank found out, he'd murdered his own son.

What about my grandmother? he said. The doctor ruled she had a heart attack. It was an accident.

She had a heart attack all right, the D.A. said. What old woman with a weak heart would not, when she came upon the sight of her great-grandson, murdered by her flesh and blood?

The D.A. charged him with murder. Frank's lawyer, sensing things were going badly, had called in an expert on post-traumatic stress disorder, right at the end of the trial. They went for a temporary insanity defense. By that time, Frank barely cared. What difference did any of it make anymore?

They gave him twenty years before parole eligibility. He served the first eight of them at the state hospital. When he was ruled competent, they moved him to the penitentiary. At the time he had jumped out the window, he had two years to go.

But I knew I had to get out of that place, he said. I knew there was some reason to jump. I wasn't wrong about that.

The reason was her. My mother. He didn't know it at the time, but he had jumped out that window to come save her.

Chapter 13

My mother asked me to go to the library for her. She and Frank wanted a book about Canada, the Maritime Provinces. Rather than all three of us going out, she figured the safest thing was just me, on my bike.

You understand, Henry, Frank said, I've got your mother here. You remember how I tied her up before. This is what is known as a hostage situation.

The way he said the words reminded me of my mother, the time a year or two after the divorce when my father had filed some kind of paper and some woman called a guardian *ad litem* came over to our house and asked my mother questions about her attitudes concerning parenthood.

Do you feel bitterness and resentment toward your ex-husband? the woman had said. Do you express your anger concerning this bitterness toward your son?

I am not bitter or angry toward my son's father, my mother told the woman. (Flat voice. Her mouth arranged in something resembling a smile.) I think he is doing a good job.

And how would you describe your attitude toward your ex-husband's wife? Your son's stepmother? Would you say you have ever impacted in a negative fashion on their relationship?

Marjorie is a nice person, my mother said. I am sure we will all be able to work together fine.

This guardian *ad litem* didn't see the part that happened after. She was gone when my mother had opened up our refrigerator and taken out the gallon milk jug from the top shelf. (Real milk. She still went grocery shopping in those days.) She didn't see my mother opening the jug and standing there in the middle of the kitchen, slowly pouring the contents on our floor, as if she were watering a pot of flowers.

Now, too, though in a different way, I had no doubt that Frank's words—*this is a hostage situation*—were what he knew he had to say at that time. Whatever else I thought about what was going on between my mother and Frank—that they were going to run away together to some fishing village in Canada, and leave me behind to live with my father and Marjorie—one thing I never

believed was that Frank had any intention of hurting my mother. Whatever he said about that, it was to
make sure we'd never get in trouble, if someone ever
found him at our house.

I won't tell, I said, playing my role of the frightened
son, as well as Frank had played his, of the heartless
convict, on the loose.

Sunday afternoon of Labor Day weekend was not
a big time at the Holton Mills library. The only reason the library was even open that day was because
they were having a book sale, all proceeds going toward the purchase of new curtains or something along
those lines. Out front on the lawn, a group of women
were selling lemonade and oatmeal cookies, and there
was a clown making balloon sculptures, with boxes of
old books for sale like some recipe collection of great
meals to make in a Crock-Pot and the autobiography
of Donny Osmond. There was a nice, cheerful mood
to the whole thing, with people milling around talking about how hot it was, mostly, and comparing notes
on what they were doing to keep cool. Not comparing notes with me, of course. It was like I gave off a
set of sound waves too high pitched for the human ear
that transmitted the message—*Stay away.* All these
happy, cheerful people munching cookies and brows-

ing through the stacks of old *Information Please* al-
manacs and *Jane Fonda Workout* books (three copies,
that I spotted) couldn't have known what was going on
back at my house, of course, but I guess I gave off the
impression of someone that wasn't interested in balloon sculptures or beach reading, which was true.

Making my way up the steps and inside the building, I was thinking I must be the only person in the
whole town who wasn't off at some cookout that day,
playing Frisbee or chopping up the potatoes for potato
salad or splashing around in a pool. It was one thing to
swing by this place for a bunch of Agatha Christies and
a lemonade. But what kind of a loser would be at the
library, researching Prince Edward Island on the last
weekend of summer before school started?

Only there was one other person. She was sitting
in the reading room, where I had come with my notebook to copy facts down from the encyclopedia—these
being the days when we still used encyclopedias to find
out about things. She was sitting in one of the leather
chairs I often sat in myself when I hung out here, only
she sat in the lotus position, as if she was meditating,
but with a book in front of her. She wore glasses and
she had her hair in a braid, and she was wearing shorts
that left a lot of her legs showing, which made it particularly obvious how skinny she was.

She looked my age, but I didn't recognize her. Normally I'd have been too shy to say anything, but maybe it was having Frank around that last couple of days— the picture of him jumping out that window, and all the other crazy stuff he'd done since, and the feeling it gave me that the world was such a crazy place you might as well just go for it—I asked the girl if she went to school around here.

I didn't before, but I just moved here, she said. I'm supposed to try out living with my dad this year. The official reason is I have an eating disorder and they're hoping a new school environment will help, but really I think my mom just wanted to get rid of me so she can fool around with her boyfriend without me getting in the way.

I know what you mean, I said. I would not have imagined I'd discuss with anyone how I'd been feeling about my mother and Frank getting together, but this girl appeared to understand, and she didn't know anybody around here, and I liked the way she looked. You couldn't call her pretty, but she gave the appearance of being a person who might care about things a lot of girls didn't, who were only interested in clothes or getting a boyfriend.

I asked her what she was reading. I'm investigating my legal rights, she said. Also child psychology.

She was doing a study of certain kinds of adolescent trauma to support her case to her parents that she was currently experiencing it.

Her name was Eleanor. Normally she lived in Chicago. Until now, she only came here for school vacations sometimes. She was going into eighth grade. She had gotten into this really great private school where they focused mainly on drama and none of the kids cared about sports and you could wear any kind of clothes you wanted or a nose ring even and the teachers didn't get on your case. But at the last minute she couldn't go.

My stupid parents said we didn't have the money, she said. So, hello Holton Mills Junior High.

I'm going into seventh grade, I said. I'm Henry.

I'd gotten a stack of books about the Maritime Provinces—the Maritimes, it turns out they were called. I had set them down on the floor next to the other leather chair, across from Eleanor's.

Are you writing a report or something? she asked.

Kind of. It's for my mother. She wants to know if Canada might be a good place to move.

Something about Eleanor made me not want to lie to her. My mother and her boyfriend, I said. I was trying out this word that I'd never used before. Not in connection to my mother anyway. There seemed to be no harm in saying it. Just because a person's mother has a boyfriend doesn't mean he's an escaped convict.

How do you feel about that? she said. Leaving your friends. I'm asking because that's what I had to do when I came here, and frankly, I consider it child abuse. Not that I'm a child, but from a legal standpoint, not to mention the psychological effects. All the experts could tell you that particularly during puberty, it is highly inadvisable for a person to have to form new bonds with new people who might or might not have anything in common with her. Especially if, no offense, she is used to living in a cosmopolitan city with things like jazz clubs and an art institute and all of a sudden the main attraction is bowling and horseshoes. When I tell my friends back home about this town, nobody can believe it. I'm not saying this applies to you, just a general impression.

I didn't feel like telling her that in my case, I didn't have any friends. Not anyone it would be hard to leave at least—just a few fellow outcasts at school, who shared the table in the cafeteria where all the losers sat, when nobody else wanted them to sit at their table. Siberia.

In my case, I said, the problem wasn't actually going away. It was getting left behind. Maybe there's some kind of trend going on in the mother community, I said. Because it seemed like my mother was also trying to get rid of me. It looked like she and her boyfriend were planning to park me with my father and his wife, Marjorie, and her son who was my age who was probably my father's favorite and their baby, who spit up on me every time they made me hold her.

I wouldn't have thought my mother would do something like this, I said.

It's sex, Eleanor said. When people have sex with each other, it affects their brain. They can't see things normally.

I might have said here that the way my mother saw things even before she started having sex with Frank was not what most people would consider normal. I was wondering if Eleanor knew about the effects of sex because she'd had sex herself, or if she'd also read this in a book. She didn't seem like someone who would have had sex yet, but she had an air of knowing a lot more than I did. If she spoke from personal experience, I didn't want to let on that I had none myself, beyond what went on in my own bed at night. Though it did support her theory when I considered how recent activities seemed to be affecting my own brain. I thought about sex almost all the time now, except when I was thinking about what was happening with my mother and Frank, but that also involved sex.

It's like they're on drugs, I said. I was thinking about a commercial they had on television. It started with a frying pan on the stove. Then you see a pair of hands holding an egg.

This is your brain, says the voice.

The hands crack the egg. The egg lands on the pan. You watch the white and yolk as they sizzle and change color.

This is your brain on drugs.

It turned out Eleanor was researching the question of whether, as a minor (she was fourteen), she could sue her parents. She was thinking about contacting a lawyer, but she wanted to read up on the basics first.

I wrote a letter to the boarding school I was going to go to, she said. To ask if they'd let me come anyway, and I could clean the bathrooms or something in exchange for the tuition. But I haven't heard back.

I told her that as soon as the bank opened on Wednesday, when I was due to start school, it looked like my mother and her boyfriend were going to withdraw all her money and drive north together. She was probably packing right now. Maybe that was the real reason they wanted me out of the house. That, or more sex.

Is your mother always, like, dating a million guys? Eleanor asked. Barhopping and answering personals ads and stuff?

Not my mom, I said. My mom is the type of person— I stopped. She was no type of person you could describe, in fact. She was like nobody on earth, just her. My mom is— I started again. I wasn't expecting this, but my voice started to crack in the middle of the sentence. I tried to make it look like I just needed to clear my throat, but it was probably obvious to Eleanor that I was upset.

You can't even blame her, she said. It's like he cast a spell on her or something. You might say he hypnotized her. These men just use their penis instead of some old watch on a chain.

I tried to look casual when she said penis. I had never known a girl who said that word out loud. My mother of course. When I had gotten poison ivy a few summers back, all over my legs and thighs, she asked if my penis was also affected, and just the summer before, when I'd tried to execute a superhero leap over a granite hitching post—but failed to clear it—she had asked, as she knelt beside me on the ground, where I was groaning and holding my crotch, to show her my penis.

I need to see if this warrants a visit to the emergency room, she said. I definitely don't want anything to jeopardize the functioning of your penis down the line, or anything to do with your testicles.

But I was used to my mother. Hearing Eleanor speak about this—a part of my own body that I'd never been able to speak of myself—seemed stranger, more intimate. Though from the moment she did, I had the sense that now we could talk about anything. We had crossed into the territory of the forbidden.

Her room's next to mine, I said. I can hear them in the night. Doing it. Her and . . . Fred.

I figured I'd call him that. To protect his identity.

So, he's a sex addict, she said. Or a gigolo. Possibly both.

Even now, I knew this wasn't so. I liked Frank. That was the problem in fact, though I didn't discuss this part. I liked him so much I had wanted to go away with him too. I liked him so much I had been picturing him becoming part of our family. These past few happy days he had been spending at our house, hanging out with my mother and me, I hadn't understood that the place he would take was mine.

You don't have some kind of Oedipus complex or anything do you? she said. Where you want to marry your mom? That sometimes happens with boys, though generally they outgrow it by your age.

I like regular girls, I told her. My age, or maybe a little older but not a lot.

If she thought I was talking about her, that was OK.

I like my mother in the mom way, I said.

In that case, you might consider an intervention, Eleanor said. That's what my mother did with me, though in my opinion they had it backwards. The person that needed the intervention was her, and her sicko boyfriend. But from a psychological perspective, it's a very effective method.

If the situation is that this person's put a kind of spell on your mom, you need to deprogram her. They did that with people who joined cults, back when that was really popular. There was a girl one time named Patty Hearst, from a rich family like the people on *Dallas,* who got kidnapped, and pretty soon the robbers, who were also political radicals and also extremely attractive, had her robbing banks.

This was back before either of us were born, Eleanor said. My mother told me about it. The man who kidnapped her had this thing called charisma, which affected her to the point that Patty Hearst started wearing army clothes and carrying a machine gun. When her parents finally got her back home, they had to send her to all sorts of psychiatrists to help her get back to her old self. It can be confusing for people, figuring out who the bad people are and who are the good ones. Or maybe nobody's really so good, which was probably why Patty Hearst got messed up with the bank robber people. She just had so many problems already, it made her vulnerable.

This would be my mother all right.

He brainwashed her with the power of sex.

If that was really the case, how would anyone get her back again? I asked. (I wasn't going to say normal. Just back to how she was before.)

Sex is too powerful, Eleanor said. Nothing you could do now would neutralize it.

In other words, the situation was hopeless. My mother was a goner. I looked at the stack of books at my feet. One was open to a photograph of a hillside on Prince Edward Island, rolling fields, ocean behind. Eleanor, when she saw the book, had pointed out that the girl in *Anne of Green Gables* lived there, but that was a whole different story. Once Frank took my mother there she'd never come back.

Just in case your parents' divorce didn't screw up your personality enough already, Eleanor said, this boyfriend business will probably leave you with major neurosis. For your sake, I hope you'll make a lot of money in the future, to pay for all the therapy you'll need.

As she spoke she was chewing on her braid, which might have been her substitute for food, it occurred to me. She had gotten up from the leather chair now so she was standing in front of me in the reading room, which made it possible for me to see that she was even skinnier than I might have imagined. She had also taken off her glasses, which revealed dark circles under her eyes. In one way, she looked really old, but also like a little girl.

I see only one hope for you, she said. I'm not saying to kill him or anything. But you need to find a way to get him out of your world.

I don't know if that's possible, I said.

Look at it this way, Hank, she said. (Hank? I had no idea where she got that.) Either you get rid of him. Or he gets rid of you. Which one is it going to be?

Back at the house, Frank and my mother were getting ready to paint the storm windows. I wouldn't have thought this would be the kind of job two people who were about to leave the country forever would be interested in, but maybe she was thinking she'd sell our place to get money for the farmhouse on Prince Edward Island. In case what she had in the bank wasn't enough. She'd want our place here looking nice.

Hey, buddy. You got back just in the nick of time, Frank said. Want to help scrape these with me?

My mother was standing next to him. She had on a pair of overalls she always used when she was working in the garden, back when we had one, with her hair tied back in a bandana. They had all our storm windows out, and a paint scraper, and some sandpaper.

What do you think? she said. I've had this paint sitting around for a couple of years now. Frank said the three of us could knock out this job in no time if we all pitched in.

I wanted to paint with them. It looked like they were having fun. She had brought the radio outside, and they were doing some kind of Labor Day weekend countdown of hits. The song on at the moment was Olivia Newton-John, doing that number from *Grease* about summer love. My mother was holding the scraper like it was a microphone, pretending to be Olivia Newton-John.

I'm busy, I said.

A hurt look came over her face.

I thought it would be a fun project for us to do together, she said. You can fill us in on what you learned at the library.

I learned that my mother had been brainwashed. That the inside of her brain, if we could see it now, under the influence of sex, would resemble a fried egg. That her only hope lay in my getting rid of Frank. I didn't say these things but I thought them.

Frank had put a hand on my shoulder now. I remembered the other time he'd done that, the first day I met him—how he'd told me he needed my help. Looking in his eyes, I had believed I could trust him.

I think you should help your mother here, son, he said.

Not angry, but firmer than I'd heard out of him before. Here it came, the thing Eleanor had warned me about. Him taking charge. Now I rode in the backseat. Soon I wouldn't be in the car at all.

You're not my boss, I said. You're not my dad.

He withdrew his hand, as if he'd touched hot metal. Or dry ice.

It's OK, Frank, my mother said. We can take care of the job, just the two of us.

I went inside and turned on the television, loud. The U.S. Open tennis match was on, not that I cared who won. One channel up, baseball. Then some infomercial for women who wanted to trim down their thighs. I didn't care that my mother and Frank would hear me watching the show—same as I heard them, through the wall in my bedroom—or that when I was finished eating my sandwich, I left the plate and my empty milk glass out on the table, instead of putting my dishes in the dishwasher the way I normally would.

I drifted over to check on Joe, still lying on the floor of his cage, panting in the heat. I got a spray bottle and rinsed it out, squirted water on his fur to cool him off, then squirted some on me.

I lay on the couch, watching the infomercial and flipping through the book I'd brought home, *Mysterious Maritimes: Land of Dreams*. I picked up the newspaper and studied the headline again. Reward offered. Ten thousand dollars.

Remove him, Eleanor said. *Get him out of your world.*

I thought about a dirt bike. A video camera. A paintball gun.

I remembered a catalog I read on the plane, coming home from Disney with my father and Marjorie, filled with all kinds of amazing things to buy that you never knew existed before, like a hoverboard and a popcorn machine to put in your own home and a clock that showed what time it was in cities all over the world and a machine that turned your bathtub into a Jacuzzi and solar-powered tiki lights and a pair of what looked like rocks, only they were really outdoor stereo speakers, made from fiberglass, for neighborhood cookouts and parties. With ten thousand dollars, a person could buy every single thing in the catalog, except for the items that weren't interesting anyway.

After they took Frank away, my mother would be sad, but she'd get over it and eventually realize it was for her own good that I did it.

Chapter 14

You probably wonder why you don't have a brother or sister, my mother said one time. This was during one of our meals together, where she liked to bring up topics to talk about while we ate our frozen dinners. I was around nine years old at the time, and I had never wondered why I didn't have a brother or sister, but I nodded anyway, understanding, even then, that this was a subject she wanted to explore with me.

I always planned on having at least two children, preferably more, she said. Having you was the first thing I did, other than dancing, where I felt I really knew what I was doing.

Six months after you were born, she said, I missed my period.

Some kids that age might not have known what their mother was talking about, if she said something along those lines. But I had lived with my mother long enough, I knew all about this. And plenty more.

I was always perfectly regular, from the day I began to menstruate, she told me. So I knew immediately what that meant. I didn't need any confirmation from a doctor.

But your father didn't want another baby so soon. He said we didn't have the money, and anyway, it bothered him how much of my time went into taking care of you, when he wanted attention for himself. Your father persuaded me to have the abortion, she said. I never wanted to do it. To me, any baby, even if it didn't come at the most convenient time, was a gift. I told your father then, it was a dangerous thing to start playing God. Waiting for things to be perfect, because they never would be.

Your father had taken me to a clinic. I had gone into the little room alone, while your father sat outside. I put on a paper gown and climbed up on the table, put my feet in the stirrups. Not the kind they have on a horse, Henry, she said.

They turned on a machine, and a noise started, like a generator, or a very large garbage disposal. She lay there, listening, while the machine kept going. The nurse said something to her but she couldn't hear, the machine was so loud. When it was over, they let her rest on a cot in a different room for a couple of hours, next to a couple of other women who had also had abortions that morning. When she came out, my father was there, though he had left in the middle, to do some shopping, she said. On the drive home she had not cried, but she stared out the window most of the way, and when he asked her, finally, what was it like? she couldn't say anything.

From the moment I had the abortion, all I wanted was to get pregnant again and have the baby this time, my mother told me. You know what I mean?

I didn't, but I nodded. To me, it made no sense that first she went through all that effort not to have a baby and the next thing you knew, she wanted one. This might be what my father meant when he asked me if I thought she was crazy.

But finally he went along with it. Just to get her off his back, he said. And for a while there, my mother was just so happy. I was just two years old at this point, which meant she was still very busy taking care of me, but though she knew women who complained about morning sickness and soreness in their breasts, or feeling tired all the time, my mother loved every single thing about being pregnant.

Somewhere near the end of her first trimester— when the fetus would have been (she knew, from her daily study of the *First Nine Months of Life* book) about the size of a lima bean—she had woken with a new and awful cramping feeling in her belly, and blood on the sheets. By midafternoon, she had gone through three sanitary napkins and the blood was still flowing.

Three sanitary napkins is a lot, Henry, she told me. I didn't know what a sanitary napkin was, but I nodded.

Her doctor, examining her, had told her it was not that unusual to miscarry and there was no reason to suppose she'd have any problems the next time. She was young. Her body looked healthy. They could try again soon.

She got pregnant again a few months later, though this time she decided to hold off wearing her maternity clothes until she was further along. She still told a few friends (this was in the days when she had friends). She also told me, though I had no memory of this. I would have been not quite three years old by this point.

Just at the end of the first trimester, again, she had begun to bleed. Sitting on the toilet—to pee, she thought—she felt something slip out of her. Looking into the toilet she'd seen what looked like a blood clot and knew she wasn't pregnant anymore. What was a person supposed to do? Flush?

After a minute of standing there, she had knelt on the floor and scooped her hand into the water. She carried the blood clot thing out into the yard and, with her fingers, tried to dig a hole, but because of the absence of topsoil, she could barely scrape the surface.

This would have been your baby brother or sister, she said.

Buried, in the backyard of the house where my father and Marjorie lived, I gathered. Though I was still thinking about the close call of almost flushing it down the toilet.

By the third time she got pregnant again, not so long after, she no longer expected things to go well, and they didn't. This time the miscarriage had come even earlier—before the two-month mark even—and she had never even felt morning sickness, which had been the first bad sign.

Now I knew God was punishing me, she said. We had been given a wonderful gift, with you, and a wonderful gift six months after your birth, and because of our own foolishness, supposing we could pick our moment to become parents, as if we were choosing when to go dancing—I knew now we might never again have the chance.

But the fourth try had seemed so much more promising. I loved it that I felt sick, she said. And then my breasts started filling out, right around the six-week mark when they were supposed to, and I was over the moon.

Don't you remember me taking you with me to the doctor that time? she said. And he showed you the ultrasound, and I said Look, there's your baby brother? Because tiny as it was we thought we could see a penis.

No, I said. I didn't remember that. There was so much to remember, sometimes the best thing was to forget.

When they had looked at the ultrasound that first time, and the doctor said everything looked good, my mother had asked him to look again, to be sure. When a few weeks later she had registered an odd feeling in her belly, she had first supposed it was the same old story unfolding again, before she realized no, this was a different one. She put her hand on her stomach and felt a strange and thrilling little ripple, like a fish passing under water, deep below the surface. She had put my hand on her belly then, so I could feel it too. My baby brother was swimming.

Then she was just so happy. We had a bad time for a while there, she had explained to me, as the two of us lay on my bed, reading my *Curious George* book.

But it's over now. This is the one that's going to be OK. I took having children for granted before. Whatever we get from here on, I'll be grateful for.

Then her labor had begun, and they set the suitcase in the car that had been packed so long ago—way back before she had the first miscarriage. Her labor had been long, but the fetal monitor had indicated a healthy heartbeat from the baby, right up until those last terrible minutes, and then suddenly they were wheeling my mother into the operating room and sending my father away. Then they were cutting her open.

Hearing this story then, at age nine, I had asked her where I was when this was happening. A friend of mine was taking care of you, she said. Not Evelyn. This was before Evelyn. Back in those days, my mother had normal people for friends.

When it was over, she could never remember much of what happened in the room that day, though she remembered hearing the words, *A girl.* Not a boy after all. A girl. But something was wrong with their voices, delivering the news. They should have sounded happy. For a moment she thought that must be the problem. Maybe the nurse thought she'd be disappointed it wasn't a son. Then she saw the nurse's face, and knew, even before she heard the words. It was something else.

Give me my baby, she had called out, but no one answered. She could see the top of the doctor's green cap, moving in hushed silence on the other side of the curtain, stitching her up. Then they must have given her some drug because soon after that she went to sleep for a long time. She did remember my father coming into the room. The important thing is you're OK, he said, though that didn't feel important at all, then, or for a long time after.

After she woke up—not right away, but soon—they had wheeled her into a room where their baby was— Fern, named for her mother, who had died so long before. Fern lay in a bassinette, like a regular baby, and she was wrapped in a pink flannel blanket. The nurses had put a diaper on her—the only one she'd ever wear.

One of the nurses set my baby sister in my mother's arms. My father was there too, in a chair next to her. They got to be alone in the room for a few minutes— long enough to fold back the blanket and study the tiny, bluish body. My mother had traced her fingers over every rib, the freshly tied knot of skin forming a belly button where the umbilical cord had been that nour- ished her all those months—and betrayed her, in the end, with that one fatal twist that cut off her oxygen. My mother took Fern's hands in hers and studied the fingernails, considered whose hands she had inher- ited. (My father's it seemed. Those same long fingers that might have inspired them to get her piano lessons later.)

She unfolded Fern's legs—no sign of the kicking she'd loved to follow, those last couple of months, so strong that sometimes she could even make out the outline of a foot, pressing against her belly from inside, making a bump. (Look, Henry, she had called to me. Didn't I remember that part? How I'd watched the person we thought was my brother moving under the skin of her belly, like a kitten under the blankets of a bed.)

She had peeled back Fern's diaper then. Knowing this was her one and only chance, she needed to see everything.

There was the small, once-pink cleft of her vagina. A dot of blood there that the doctor would explain later was not uncommon in newborn baby girls—result of hormones passing from mother to child—though when they'd seen it, they drew in their breath.

My mother memorized her face in the space of those few minutes, knowing how many times over the years she would think back on this time, and what she would give then (anything) to hold this baby again as she did now.

Her eyes were closed. She had long, surprisingly dark lashes (even darker looking against the blue-white of her skin). Her nose was not the button some babies have, but more of a miniature adult nose, with a strong, straight bridge and two tiny, perfectly formed nostrils, drawing no breath. Her mouth a flower. A tiny cleft in her chin, my father's, again, though her jawline seemed to belong to my mother's side of the family.

There was one blue vein visible, beneath the skin, traversing the area between her jaw and down her small, limp neck. My mother traced it all the way along her body.

I was like a river guide, she said, pointing out to some traveler the route to follow. The vein was still visible as my mother's finger made its way along Fern's chest, and toward the spot where, just below the thin, almost translucent skin, a tiny heart whose rhythms she had felt inside her all this time now rested still as stone.

All this she described to me, as if it was a story she knew so well she was not so much telling it as reciting it, though very likely I was the only person she'd ever told it to.

After a while, a nurse had come back in the room and lifted Fern out of my mother's arms. My father pushed the wheelchair back to the room. In the hall, they had passed a couple heading toward the elevator with a new baby and a bouquet of helium balloons, and a woman with a hospital gown billowing over her huge belly—in the early stages of labor. Just like herself, less than eighteen hours earlier, this pregnant woman paced the hall, filling the time between those early and irregularly spaced contractions. Seeing her, my mother said, a crazy thought had come to her. *Give me another chance. I'll do it right next time.* This was the first time, but hardly the last, that the sight of a pregnant woman had taken my mother to a place of so much anger and grief that simply breathing had felt impossible. There would be pregnant women everywhere now. More than there ever used to be was how it seemed.

As they made their way across the parking lot to their car, my father had bent over the chair, as if he was shielding my mother from a gale force wind. It will be better once we get home, Adele, he told her.

It wasn't really, though by the time he brought her back to the house—the house he lived in now with Marjorie, and the baby girl he and Marjorie had together later, who lived—he had cleared out the nursery, packed up the boxes of baby clothes and newborn Pampers (some of them purchased three years earlier), and dismantled the crib.

After the first miscarriage, and the second, my parents had talked about trying again. Even after the third—though a sense of dread had taken hold in them—they still met with the doctor and marked the calendar with the dates of my mother's periods and notations for her fertile times.

After they buried Fern, no further discussion took place concerning conception, pregnancy, or babies.

Their friends had offered condolences, and made efforts to include them in the social life of the neighborhood, but now my mother learned not to attend neighborhood barbecues and school events. Someone was always pregnant. The supermarket was dangerous too. More maternity tops, and baby food, and babies in the shopping carts, the age that Fern would be, and toddlers, the age of the one before her, and four-year-olds, the age of the one they'd buried in the yard. Wherever you looked, pregnant women and babies, as if it was an epidemic.

Pretty soon my mother understood: no place was safe anymore. Babies and the promise of babies were everywhere. Just opening your window, you might hear one crying. Once, lying in bed, she had been awakened by the faint cry of some neighborhood baby. It only lasted a few moments. The mother must have picked him up. Or the father did. But it was too late for sleep after that. My mother had lain there in the dark the rest of the night, going over it all again. The abortion. The miscarriages. The ultrasound. The foot pressing out under the fabric of her shirt. The twisted cord. The dot of blood. The tiny box of ashes they'd given her, no bigger than a pack of cigarettes.

After that morning, she knew, she was done going out in the world. She wasn't interested in making love with her husband anymore, and giving birth to any more dead babies. She didn't even care about dancing. The only safe place was home.

Chapter 15

It was the middle of the afternoon when my mother and Frank came in from painting. My mother was running a bath. Even though I was still mad at her, I called out to her, asking what was for lunch. Frank came in the room, not her.

How about I fix us some chow? he said. Give your mother a chance to take it easy. She's been working hard.

Yeah, right, I thought. *I heard you two in the night. Who made her work hard anyway?*

Upstairs, I could hear the sound of water running. Frank had stripped off his shirt, that had paint on it. He was bare-chested. His pants were loose around his hips, hanging low enough that the top of his bandage was visible, from where they'd cut out his appendix, but otherwise, he could have been a statue. Even though he was old, he had that type of chest where all the bones are held in with muscles. I thought again, the way I did when I met him, of how he was the type of person that you could picture as a skeleton, or lying on a table, getting dissected. All the parts of him were so clearly defined by muscle and bone, with no fat covering them. He didn't look like a bodybuilder or a superhero or anything like that. He looked like the illustration in a biology book, for a page they'd label *Man*.

I was thinking we could throw around the ball for a bit, he said. Me being sweaty already, I might as well get more so, and my ankle's feeling strong enough to stand on for longer now. I want to see how your arm's looking.

This was difficult. I wanted him to know I felt mad, and left out, and that I was onto his tricks with my mother, if that's what they were. But I couldn't help liking him. I was also bored. On the television now, Jerry Lewis was standing at a microphone pretending to talk like a little kid to a girl who was standing next to him on the stage, with braces on her legs and a walker.

What do you say, friends? Jerry Lewis was saying, in the fake little-kid voice. Doesn't Angela deserve a chance like the rest of us? Get out your checkbooks.

I had liked it when Frank played catch with me. I wasn't expecting him to turn me into some kind of

overnight jock, but it felt good throwing the ball back
and forth, the thwack of it, when it landed in my glove.
The rhythm we had going, him to me, me to him, him
to me.

I never realized it before, my mother had said, when
she joined us, but playing catch is sort of like dancing.
You have to tune in to the other person and focus totally on their moves, then adapt your own to the other
person's timing. Like when you're out on the floor with
your partner and the whole world is just the two of you,
communicating perfectly even though no one says anything.

When he threw me the ball, I didn't think he was
picturing having sex with her, or kissing that place on
her neck where the mark was, or her lying naked upstairs in the bathtub, or any of the other things that
went on at night in her bed. When we played catch, he
was just thinking about playing catch.

Either that, or he was hypnotizing me also. Maybe
he was even trying to prepare me for the day, very
soon, when I'd be living at my father's house, and my
father and Richard would be out there playing catch all
the time, only unlike me, Richard could throw a cur-
veball. He was preparing me for the future, when he
and my mother would be gone.

I guess not, I told him. I'm watching a show. Meaning the telethon.

Frank's eyes didn't leave my face. Jerry Lewis didn't exist. Just him and me, in that room.

Listen, he said. If you're worried I'm going to steal your mother, forget it. There would never be a day you aren't numero uno in her book, and I would never try and change that. She's always going to love you more than anything. I'd just like to be the person who takes care of her, for a change. I won't try to be your dad. But I could be a friend.

Here it came. Just what Eleanor warned me about. Now he was going to try and hypnotize me too. I could even feel how it worked, because part of me wanted to believe him. I had to drown out the words, so they wouldn't seep into my brain.

The girl was sitting on Jerry Lewis's lap, talking about her puppy. A phone number was up on the screen. Down the block, I could hear voices from the Jervises' aboveground pool. *Blah blah blah,* I told myself. *Blahdy, blahdy, blah.*

I know I haven't done a very good job up until now, he said. I made terrible mistakes. But if I ever got another chance somehow, I'd never stop working to make it right.

Jaboolah, kazoolah, banana.

Ravioli. Stromboli. Holey moley.

I also know it takes time, he said. Look at me. All I've had these last eighteen years was time. The one good thing, it gives a person the opportunity to think.

He stood there with the paint scraper. He was wearing a pair of old pants my mother had found in the basement, from a Halloween costume she made me a few years earlier, where I'd dressed up as a clown. The pants must have belonged to a very fat person; they'd been way too big for me, which was the point, but on Frank they only came to the middle of his calves, and he was holding them up with a piece of rope. He had the same shirt on from when we met him—the one that said Vinnie—and no shoes. He looked like a clown himself, actually, just not the funny kind. This was the person I could hear kissing my mother on the other side of the wall every night. I felt bad for her. Bad for him also. Bad for myself the most. I had always wanted to be in a real family and here I was, in a family of losers.

Now he put his hand on my shoulder. A big, worn hand. I had heard my mother saying to him, through the wall at night, I'll put some lotion on your skin.

Your skin's so smooth, he said. I feel ashamed to touch you.

Now he was talking to me, though in a different voice. We don't have to play ball, either. I could just make us something to eat. Sit out on the back step. It might be cooler there.

My dad's picking me up later, I said.

And I know what you and my mother will do the minute I'm out the door.

From upstairs I could hear my mother, calling through the bathroom door. Can you bring me a towel, Frank?

He got up then. He turned to face me, with a look on his face like he might have had when Mandy answered his question about who the real father of the baby was, except this time he wasn't going to push anyone or knock them so hard their head broke. He had told me he was a patient man now. Patient enough to wait for his opportunity, hold out whole years for the moment when he'd finally found himself in a hospital bed, next to a second-story window without bars on it. His plan might take a while, but he had put it into motion.

Now he was lifting a bath towel from the stack of laundry on top of the machine, raising it to his face, smelling it, as if he wanted to make sure it was good enough for her skin. Now he was climbing the stairs. Now I heard the door opening. Now he would be standing next to the tub where my mother lay. Naked.

Back at the library, Eleanor had written down her phone number at her father's house. I'll be there all weekend, she'd told me. Unless my dad gets some idea to take me to the movies or something. Knowing him he probably still thinks I'd consider *The Care Bears* movie a thrill.

I dialed the number. If her father answered, I'd hang up.

But she did. I was hoping you'd call, she said. What kind of a girl said something like that?

Want to talk? I said.

Chapter 16

That afternoon, the temperature reached ninety-five. The air had a heaviness to it. Up and down the street, people were watering their lawns. Not us. Our grass was dead already.

The paper that morning featured an article about gypsy moths and an interview with a woman who had started a campaign to institute the policy of school uniforms at public school, on the theory that they would cut down on peer pressure and inappropriate clothing on the part of teenagers. Young people should be thinking about their math homework at school, she said. Not some girl's legs sticking out from under a miniskirt.

It wouldn't matter if they put the girls in uniforms, I wanted to tell her. You didn't think about their clothes. You thought about what was under them. Rachel

McCann could be wearing saddle shoes and a kilt down to her ankles. I'd still be picturing her breasts.

Eleanor was so thin, it was difficult picturing her body. It had been hard to get an idea about her chest, because she'd been wearing a bulky sweatshirt at the library. (A sweatshirt. In the middle of a heat wave.)

Still, I thought about what she'd look like with her glasses off. I pictured her taking the elastic band off her braid, her hair hanging loose on her shoulders. Her chest, naked, if we were pressed against each other, probably wouldn't feel all that different from mine. The picture came to me of the two of us, lining our nipples up so they touched each other, as if that might make an electrical connection. We were about the same height. All the places on our bodies could match up, except for the one, where we'd be different.

There is a theory that girls develop eating disorders as a way of avoiding their sexuality, she had told me. Certain psychologists believe that if a person has an eating disorder, that's their way of trying to hold on to their childhood, because they're scared of what the next phase would be like. You don't get your period if you're very thin, for instance. I know most people wouldn't tell a boy that kind of thing, but I think people should always be honest when they talk to each other. Like, if my mother needed to be alone with her boyfriend, she could have just told me. I would have gone over to my friend's house for a sleepover or something, instead of having to move halfway across the country so they could have sex.

On the phone that afternoon, she asked what kind of music I liked. She liked this singer called Sid Vicious, and the Beastie Boys. She thought Jim Morrison was the coolest person ever. Someday, she wanted to go to Paris and visit his grave.

I figured I should know who Jim Morrison was, so I didn't say anything. All we had at my house was my mother's cassette player that had an am radio. Mostly I only knew the music she listened to: Frank Sinatra ballads and the original sound track to *Guys and Dolls* and a Joni Mitchell album called *Blue* and a man I didn't know the name of, with a very low sleepy voice. He had this one song she used to play over and over again. There was a line in it: *And you know that she's half crazy but that's why you want to be there.*

She's touched your perfect body with her mind, he sang. You couldn't call it singing exactly. More like chanting. I figured Eleanor might like this singer if I could remember his name but I couldn't.

You know, the usual, I told her, when she asked about the music.

I never like the usual, she said. Not the usual anything.

She had asked me if I had a bike. I did, but it was meant for an eight-year-old and had a flat tire and we didn't have a pump. She didn't have a bike, but she could borrow her father's. He was off playing golf or something. Here was a person who said he didn't have money to send his daughter to the best school in the universe and he spent fifty dollars every weekend, hitting a ball around and trying to get it in the hole.

I could come over to your house, she said.

That might not be the greatest idea, I told her. My mother and the man were keeping a low profile. *Fred.*

We could meet up in town, she said. We could go out for coffee.

I didn't tell her that I didn't drink coffee. I said that sounded good. This was in the days before they had places like Starbucks, but there was a diner called Noni's, where they had individual booths, and every booth had a box installed next to it, where you could flip through all the different songs on their jukebox. Mostly country, but there might be something she'd like. Some very sad song, where the person sounded depressed.

It was a twenty-minute walk to town. When I left, my mother and Frank were still upstairs in the bathroom. He must have been drying her off, or putting lotion on her skin. I just want to take care of your mother, he'd said. That's what he called it.

I left them a note to say I'd be back in time for when my dad came by. I'm meeting up with a friend, I said. That would make my mother happy.

Eleanor was in a booth already when I got to the diner. She'd changed out of her shorts, and her hair was down loose the way I'd pictured it, though in real life it turned out to be sort of straight and spiky, not curly the way I'd imagined it. She had makeup on— purplish lipstick and a line around her eyes that made them look even bigger than they were. She had black nail polish on her fingernails, but they were bitten down, which was an odd combination.

She said, I told my dad I was getting together with a boy. He started giving me this lecture about being careful, like I was going to jump in bed with you or something.

It's funny how parents are always giving you these talks about sex, like that's all that goes on in our lives. When they're probably just projecting their own obsessions, she said.

She poured a Sweet'N Low into her coffee. Then two more. My dad doesn't have a girlfriend, but he wishes he did, she told me. He could probably be attractive if he'd lose weight. Too bad he and your mom didn't get together before this Fred person showed up. You could have been my stepbrother. Of course then if we got married, it would be kind of like incest.

My mother doesn't normally date, I told her. What happened with this guy was a fluke situation.

We sat there for a minute, not saying anything. She put another five or six packets of Sweet'N Low in her coffee. I tried to think up a topic.

Can you believe about the escaped convict? she said. My dad was talking about it with our next-door neighbor who's a state trooper. I guess the police have this theory that he might still be in the area because they've had all these roadblocks up on account of the holiday weekend, and they figure they would have spotted him if he tried to get out of town. Of course he could have hidden in someone's trunk or something like that, but they think he might be holed up someplace till he recuperates from his injuries. They're pretty sure he must have broken his leg, at least, when he jumped out the window.

Even if he's around, I said, he might not be so bad. He's probably just trying to mind his own business.

Even now, as bad as I felt about him stealing my mom, it was uncomfortable hearing someone talk about Frank like he was a terrible person. In a funny way, even though I'd started wishing he'd just disappear,

I couldn't really blame him for wanting to get together with my mother. All the things he was doing with her were what I wished I could do with some girl myself.

I don't know why people are so worked up, I said. He probably isn't dangerous.

I guess you don't read the paper, she said. They had an interview in it, with the sister of the woman he killed. Not only that, but he killed his own baby.

Sometimes there's more of a story than they put in the newspaper, I said. I would have liked to explain to her about Mandy laughing at Frank, and how she'd tricked him to marry her and think Francis Junior was his son when really he wasn't, even though he ended up loving him just as much anyway. Only I couldn't say these things, so I just sat there, flipping through the pages on the jukebox remote, looking for some song that might set the mood.

Some cashier over at Pricemart saw him. She called up the hotline, after she saw his picture. He was with some woman and a kid. Hostages most likely. She was hoping to get the reward, but just seeing him wasn't enough. It's the first interesting thing that happened in this town since my mother exiled me here.

I know where he is, I told her. My house.

After I paid the bill—mine and hers—we walked outside the diner, and over to the video store. There was this movie she said I should see called *Bonnie and Clyde*, about a criminal who kidnaps a beautiful woman and gets her to start robbing banks with him. Unlike Patty Hearst, Bonnie wasn't rich, but she was restless and bored, same as my mother must have been at the point Frank came along, she said, and like my mother she hadn't had any sex in a long time probably. And Clyde had all this charisma, same as the man in the Patty Hearst situation.

Warren Beatty, she said. Now he's pretty old, but back when they made the movie he was the handsomest man ever. My mother said that even in real life he had that charisma type of effect on people. He was always getting women in Hollywood to sleep with him even if they knew he was sleeping with other people too. They couldn't help it.

In the movie, Bonnie and Clyde fell in love. They drove all around the place, holding up banks and stores and living out of their car. The odd thing was, Clyde couldn't even have sex with Bonnie. He had some kind of phobia about that, but even without actually doing it, she still lost her perspective, just from the sex appeal. In the end they got killed. This person they thought was their friend, who was part of their gang, betrayed them to keep from going to prison.

There's this scene at the end of the movie where the federal agents track them down and ambush them, Eleanor said. The part where Bonnie gets killed, there's so much blood my mother couldn't even watch it on the video, but I did. It wasn't even like a single shot that got her. They had these machine guns, and her body started jumping all around the seat of the car going into spasms, while the bullets keep hitting her in new places, and you could see the blood seeping through her dress.

Bonnie was played by Faye Dunaway, she said. She's very striking. In the movie, she wore amazing clothes. Not so much the dress she had on when they shot her, but some of her other outfits.

I don't think it would be a very good idea, me renting this movie, I told Eleanor. If my mother and Frank saw me watching it, they might get the wrong idea.

I didn't actually want to see it myself, anyway. Thinking about the scene she described, where Bonnie gets shot, I knew I'd be more like Eleanor's mother. Especially since it might bring to mind the current situation.

Can you imagine if your mom got killed in an ambush? Eleanor said. And you were right there watching it. They probably wouldn't shoot at you since you're a kid, but you'd see the whole thing. It could be extremely traumatic.

We were still standing outside the video store when she said this. A woman walked past, pushing a stroller. A man dropped a movie in the slot. The heat seemed to be radiating from the sidewalk. *Hot enough to fry an egg,* I'd heard somebody say one time. *Like the tits on a Las Vegas showgirl. Your brain on drugs.* We had only been out of the air-conditioning a few minutes and already my shirt was sticking to my skin.

Eleanor had put her sunglasses on—very large, round sunglasses that covered half her face, and for a minute she just looked at me, though the sunglasses were so dark I couldn't see her eyes. Then she reached out one long thin arm and touched my face. Her wrist was as thin as a broom handle. With a ballpoint pen, probably, she had drawn a dotted line, and the words written on her skin, *Cut here.*

I have this really weird feeling, Eleanor said. There's this thing I keep wanting to do only you'd think I was strange, but I don't even care.

I don't think you're strange, I said. I tried not to ever lie, but this was an exception.

She took off her glasses and folded them into her shoulder bag. She looked around briefly. She licked her lips. Then she leaned over and kissed me.

I bet you never did that before, she said. Now you'll always remember, I was the first girl you ever kissed.

208 • JOYCE MAYNARD

It was almost five o'clock when I got home. My mother and Frank were sitting on the back porch drinking lemonade. Her shoes were off and she was holding a bottle of nail polish. Her legs were stretched out across his lap and he was painting her toenails red.

Your father called, my mother told me. He'll be over in half an hour. I was starting to get worried you might not make it back in time.

I told her I'd be ready and went upstairs to take a shower. Frank's razor was there now. Also the shaving cream. A few black hairs circling the place where the water drained out. This was what it felt like, having a man in the house.

I wondered if they'd taken a shower together while I was gone. People did that in movies. I pictured him coming up behind her, putting his arm around her neck, kissing her in that place he left the mark. His tongue in her mouth the way Eleanor had put her tongue in mine.

Water running down her face. Running off her breasts. She put her hand on him. That place I was touching now, on my own body.

I thought about Eleanor, and Rachel, and Ms. Evenrud, my social studies teacher from last year, who left the top two buttons on her shirt unbuttoned.

I thought about Kate Jackson on *Charlie's Angels* and a time I was at the town pool when a girl who was someone's babysitter had come out of the water with the two-year-old and didn't notice the top of her bathing suit had gotten pulled down, so part of her nipple showed.

The noises Frank and my mother made in the night. Imagining that it was my bed banging against the wall, not hers. Eleanor in it, only a less skinny version of her. This one had breasts that rounded out, not a lot, but slightly. As I touched them, that song my mother always played was coming through the wall.

Suzanne takes you down to her place near the river.

There was a way of listening to music where, in one way or another, practically every single thing they sang was about sex. There was a way of looking at the world where practically every single thing that happened had some kind of double meaning.

I could hear Frank outside, washing the paintbrushes. When my father came by, he'd lie low. Not that my father ever stayed long. I tried to be out the door before he even made it to the front step, to keep the two of them—my father and my mother—from saying anything to each other. Or not saying anything, which was what usually happened, which was the worst.

Normally, I would have just wrapped a towel around my waist and walked through the hall to my room that way. But with Frank here, I felt shy about my thin, unmuscled chest, my narrow shoulders. He could pick me up and crush me if he wanted.

I could crush him too. A different way.

When are you going to call them? Eleanor asked me. The police.

Later I guess. I have to think about it.

I wished I didn't, but I couldn't get the picture out of my head, of my mother sitting at the kitchen table, him setting the coffee next to her. No big deal. He had just buttered the biscuit for her, though carefully. Doing that thing he showed us, pulling it apart instead of slicing, so there was more surface area for the butter to sink in. When she took a bite, a small dot of jam had stuck to her cheek. He had dipped his napkin in his water glass and dabbed the spot. Her eyes, when he touched her, had this look. Like a person who's been wandering in the desert a long time, and finally, there's water.

Breakfast, he said. Who needs anything more than this?

Remember this moment, she said.

Chapter 17

My father and Marjorie had bought a minivan, where the back door slid open instead of swinging out the way it did on our old station wagon. This type of vehicle had only recently come on the market, which meant my father and Marjorie had been on a waiting list for a couple of months before one became available. When it did, the model that showed up at the Dodge dealership had been a kind of maroon color that Marjorie didn't like. She wanted white, because an article she'd read someplace had reported that white cars were the least likely to get into accidents.

Richard and Chloe are my precious cargo, she said. There had been a pause before she added what came next. And Henry of course.

In the end they took the maroon one. Your father has a perfect driving record, Marjorie pointed out, as if any of us was worried about getting killed on the highway. In my case, my worries had more to do with not going out in cars. Staying home all the time was the worry. Not that going to Friendly's with my father and Marjorie was my idea of a great outing.

They always pulled up in front of my mother's house at five thirty on the dot. I was waiting on the front step for them. This time, in particular, I didn't want to risk my father coming all the way up the walk to the door and seeing inside.

Richard was sitting in the back next to Chloe in her car seat, listening to a CD with headphones on. He didn't look up when I got in, but Chloe did. She had started to say a few words by this time. She had a piece of banana in her hand, that she was partly eating and mostly smearing over her face.

Give your brother a kiss, kidlets, Marjorie said.

That's OK, I told her. It's the thought that counts.

What do you think about this heat, son? my father said. Good thing we went for the aircon option on the Caravan. A weekend like this, all I want to do is stay in the car.

Smart thinking, I said.

How's your mother doing, Henry? Marjorie said. The voice she used when she asked about my mother sounded like she was asking about a person who had cancer.

Great, I told her.

If there was one person in the universe I didn't feel like filling in on the topic of my mother, Marjorie was it.

Now that school's starting, it would be a great time for your mom to find a job, Marjorie said. With all the college kids going back to school and so forth. Waitressing a few nights a week or something along those lines. Just to get her out of the house a bit. Bring in a little cash.

She has a job already, I said.

I know. The vitamins. I was thinking, maybe something a little more dependable.

So, son, my father said. Seventh grade. How about that?

There wasn't much to say, so I didn't.

Richard's been thinking of going out for lacrosse this season, haven't you, Rich? my father said.

In the seat next to me, Richard was nodding his head to some song none of the rest of us could hear. If he knew my father had asked him a question, he gave no sign.

How about you, old pal? my father continued. Lacrosse could be good. Then there's soccer. Probably not football, until you put a little more meat on those bones, huh?

Probably not football anytime in the next century, I said. Probably not lacrosse either.

I was thinking about signing up for the modern dance group, I told him.

Just to see his reaction.

I'm not sure that would be such a good move, my father said. I know how your mother feels about dancing, but people might get the wrong idea about you.

Wrong idea?

What your father's trying to say is, they might think you were gay, Marjorie said.

Or they might just think I wanted to hang around a lot of girls in leotards, I told her. Richard looked up when I said that, which made me think he'd probably been hearing everything. He just preferred to stay out of it, which was understandable.

We had reached Friendly's now. Richard jumped out his side of the van.

Can you get your sister for me? Marjorie said.

I had figured out some time ago that this was part of her strategy for fostering a relationship between me and Chloe.

Maybe you should take her, I said. I think she's got something in her diaper.

I always ordered the same thing: a hamburger and fries. Richard got a cheeseburger. My father got a steak.

Marjorie, who watched her weight, got the Healthy Living Special of a salad and fish.

So, are you munchkins looking forward to being back in school? she said.

Not particularly.

But once things get started you'll get into the swing of things. See all your friends again.

Yup.

Before you know it, you two boys will probably start going out on dates, she said. A couple of lady-killers like you. If I was still in seventh grade, I'd think you were the cutest.

Gross, Mom, said Richard. Anyway, if you were still in seventh grade, I wouldn't be born. Or if I was, and you thought I was so cute, that would be incest.

Where do they learn these words? Marjorie said.

She had a whole other voice talking to my father than the one she used for Richard and Chloe and me, which was also a different voice from the one she used when the topic of my mother came up.

Marjorie's got a point, my father said. You two are reaching that stage of life. The wild and wonderful world of puberty, so they say. The time is probably coming for us to have a little man-to-man talk about all of that.

I had that already, with my real dad, Richard said.

That just leaves you and me then, I guess, son, my father said.

It's OK, I told him. I'm up to speed.

I'm sure your mother's given you the basics, but there are some things a guy needs to find out from a man. It can be difficult if you don't have a man around the house.

There is one, I yelled, but in my head. It can also be difficult if you do have a man around the house, if he's banging the headboard of your mother's bed up against the wall every night. If he's in the shower with her. They were probably home at this very moment, doing it.

The waitress came over with the dessert menus and cleared away our plates.

Isn't this great? Marjorie said. Getting the whole family around the table like this. You boys getting to spend time together.

Richard had his headphones on again. Chloe had her hand on my ear. She was pulling it.

So who's got room for a sundae? my father said.

Only he and the baby did, though hers mostly ended up on her face. I was already thinking about how they would want me to kiss her good-bye when we got back to the house. I would have to find a spot where there wasn't any chocolate sauce, like the back of her head or her elbow. And then get out of there as quickly as possible.

Frank was washing the dishes when I got back in the house. My mother was sitting at the kitchen table with her feet on a chair.

Your mother's some kind of dancer, he said. I couldn't keep up with her. Most people wouldn't try the Lindy in this weather. But most people aren't her.

Her shoes—her dancing shoes—lay on the floor under the table. Her hair looked damp—maybe from the dancing, maybe from living. She was drinking a glass of wine, but when I came in the room she set it down.

Come here. I want to talk to you.

I wondered if she'd been reading my thoughts. For so long it had been just the two of us, maybe she'd figured out what I'd been thinking about, my plan. Maybe she knew what I'd been talking about with Eleanor, the call to the hotline. I would deny everything, but my mother would know the truth.

For a moment I imagined what would happen then. Frank tying me up. Not with scarves: with rope, or duct tape, or possibly a combination. I couldn't really imagine my mother letting Frank do something like that, except that Eleanor said when sex entered into the picture, everything changed. Look at Patty Hearst, robbing that bank, even though her parents back home were rich. Look at those hippie women who got hooked up with Charles Manson and before you knew it they were slaughtering pigs and murdering people. It was sex that pushed them all over the edge.

Frank has asked me to marry him, she said.

I know it's an unusual situation. There are some problems. It isn't news to any of us that life is complicated.

I understand you haven't known me long, Henry, Frank said. You could have the wrong impression. I wouldn't blame you if you did.

After your father left, my mother said, I was thinking I'd be on my own forever. I didn't think I'd ever care about anyone else again, she said. Anyone besides you. I wasn't expecting I could ever feel hopeful about anything ever again.

I'd never get between you and your mother, Frank said. But I think we could be a family.

I wanted to ask how that was supposed to happen, with them off on Prince Edward Island and me having dinner every night with my father and Marjorie and her precious cargo who were too good to ride in any car unless it was white? I wanted to say, Maybe you'd better think about what happened, the last time this guy had a family, Mom. Seems like his record's not so great in the family department.

But even then, mad as I was, as well as scared, I knew that wasn't fair. Frank wasn't a murderer. I just didn't want him to take my mother away and leave me.

We have to go away, my mother said. We'd have to live under a different identity. Start over with different names.

Him and her, in other words. The two of them. Disappearing.

The truth was, I'd dreamed about doing that. Sometimes, sitting at the Siberia table at school, I had imagined how it would be if NASA asked for volunteers to go live on some whole different planet, or we'd join the Peace Corps, or go work with Mother Teresa in India, or we joined the Witness Protection Program where we'd get plastic surgery to change our faces and identity cards with all new names on them. They'd tell my father I died in a tragic fire. He'd be sad but he'd get over it. Marjorie would be happy. No more child support.

We're thinking Canada would be good, she said. They speak English, and we don't need passports to get across the border. I have a little money. Actually, Frank does too, from his grandmother's property, only if he tried to get at it they'd find him so we can't touch that.

All this time, I hadn't said anything. I was looking at her hands. Remembering how she used to rub the top of my head when we sat on the couch together. She reached out to touch my hair now too, but I pushed her away.

That's great, I said. Have a wonderful trip. I guess I'll see you around. Sometime in the future, huh?

What are you talking about? she said. We're all going away, you big dope. How could I ever live without you?

So I'd been wrong that they were leaving me. To hear her talk, we were going on this big adventure together, the three of us. Eleanor had put a bunch of crazy ideas in my head. I should have known better.

Unless this was a trick. Maybe my mother didn't even know, herself, if it was. This could be Frank's way of getting her to come with him—saying I'd be coming later, only I never would. All of a sudden, I didn't know what to believe anymore. I didn't know what was real. Though this much was for sure: my mother's hands weren't shaking like usual.

You'd have to leave your school, my mother said, as if this would be hard for me. You can't tell anyone where you were going. We'd just pack the car and head out on the road.

What about the roadblocks? The highway patrol? The photographs in the paper, and on the news?

They're looking for a man traveling alone, she said. They won't expect to see a family.

There was the word again that got me every time. I studied her face, to see if I could detect any sign of a lie. I looked at Frank then, still washing dishes.

Until this moment, I hadn't noticed, but he looked different. He had the same face, of course, and the same tall, lean, muscled body. But his hair, that had been brown and gray, was all black now. Dyed. Even his eyebrows. He looked a little like Johnny Cash. I knew his records from back when Evelyn and Barry used to come over. For some reason, Barry loved *Live from Folsom Prison*, so we had played it all the time.

Now I pictured the three of us on an island somewhere—Prince Edward Island, come to think of it. My mother would have a flower garden and play her cello. Frank would paint people's houses and fix things. At night, he'd cook for us, and after dinner, in our little farmhouse, we'd sit around and play cards. It would be all right that the two of them slept together. I would be older. I'd have a girlfriend of my own, and go off in the woods with her, or out on some bluff by the ocean, where the Gulf Stream flowed by. When she came out of the water, naked, I'd hold the towel for her and dry her off.

I need to ask your permission, Frank said. You are your mother's whole family. We'd need your OK on this.

She was holding his hand as he spoke. But she was holding mine also, and for that moment at least, it seemed possible, seemed to make sense even, that a person could love her son and love her lover, and nobody would come up short. We'd all be happy. Her being happy was only a good thing for me. Our finding each other—not just him finding her, but all three of us—was the first true piece of good luck in any of our lives in a long time.

Yes, I said. It's OK with me. Canada.

Chapter 18

You wouldn't have thought it could get any hotter, but it did. That night was so hot, I didn't even put a sheet on top of myself, I just lay on top of the bed in my boxers, with a wet rag on my stomach and a glass of ice water next to the bed. I would have thought my mother and Frank would take a night off from their usual activities, but if anything, the heat just seemed to make them more crazed than ever.

The other nights, they had seemed to have waited until they thought I was asleep before they started, but maybe because they'd talked to me about getting married and all of us going to Canada together—because I'd given them my blessing, you might say—they started in before I even had my light turned off.

Adele. Adele. Adele.

Frank.

His low growling Johnny Cash voice. Hers, soft and breathless. First soft, then louder. Then the headboard against the wall. Her bird cry. His, like a dog that was having a dream about a bone someone gave him once, reliving how it felt, sucking out the juice.

Lying there in the damp heat, the air so still the curtains didn't move, I thought about Eleanor, to get my mind off things. Except for how skinny she was, she was pretty. Or maybe not pretty, but there was a kind of energy field around her. You could imagine getting an electric shock just from touching her, but not necessarily in a bad way. When she kissed me, she tasted like Vicks VapoRub. Eucalyptus. She had put her tongue in my ear.

She was also a little crazy, but this might have been good news. If she was a regular girl she'd understand— or if she didn't yet she'd find out soon—that being friends with me would be a poor strategic move for establishing her own social standing at our school. I had pointed this out to her already at the library, but she just looked at me.

You might not want to be seen talking to me once school starts, I told her. The popular kids will think you're a loser.

She said, Why would I want to be friends with those people?

Now I imagined the two of us kissing some more, only not standing up this time. Lying down. She had her hands on my head and her fingers were raking through my hair. She was like a stray cat, underfed and skittish, with a kind of forest wildness. She might run away. Or she could pounce. You never knew if she would lick your face or run her claws over your skin and draw blood.

I pictured her pulling her shirt off. She didn't even wear a bra. No need. But her breasts, which I had assumed were totally flat, actually curved up slightly off her chest, and she had small pink nipples that stood out more than you'd think, like push pins.

You can kiss them, she said.

In the next room, that was what Frank and my mother were doing, probably, but I didn't want to think about it, so I tuned back in to the Eleanor channel.

Where would you like me to put my mouth? she said.

In the morning, the coffee smell. Frank had found some wild blueberries in the scrub at the end of our yard, that he used for pancakes. Too bad we don't have maple syrup, he said. Back on the farm with his grandparents, they had tapped their trees and boiled it in a sap house every March. Some they boiled down for maple cream that they spread on the biscuits.

I'll work so hard once we get to Canada, he said. I want you to have everything. A nice kitchen. A porch. A high bed with a window looking out to some rolling fields. Next summer, I'll plant a garden.

You and me, buddy, he said. We can get some serious baseball time in. Come spring, I'll have you so you could field a bullet if it landed in your glove.

There is a certain kind of scene they have in movies, to show people falling in love. *Butch Cassidy and the Sundance Kid* would be a good example, but there are plenty more. Instead of going through all the particulars, they just play some catchy romantic song and while it's going, you're seeing the two people having all this fun together: riding bicycles and running through a field holding hands, or eating ice cream, or going around on a carousel. They're in a restaurant and he's feeding her spaghetti off his fork. They're in a rowboat, and it tips over, but when their heads come up out of the water they're laughing. Nobody drowns. Everything's perfect, and even when things get messed up like the boat tipping over, there's something perfect about that too.

That day, you could have made one of those movie segments about us, only instead of two people falling in love it would be three people, turning into a family.

Corny but true, starting with the pancakes and going on from there.

After we cleared the dishes, Frank and I played catch again for a while, and he told me how much better I was getting, which was true. Then my mother came out, and we washed the car together, and just as we were finishing up, she turned the hose on Frank and me, so we got soaked, but because of how hot it was, that just felt good. Then Frank took the hose from my mother and squirted water onto her, which got her so wet she had to go in and change, and she told us to come in and wait downstairs, and she put on this fashion show. Really the fashion show was for Frank, but I liked seeing it too—the way she sashayed around the room in one outfit after another, like a model on a runway, or a girl in the Miss America pageant.

A lot of the clothes she put on to show him were things I'd never seen her wear, probably because she'd never had the occasion. You could tell he loved it and in a different way from him, I did too. She was so pretty, I felt proud of her. I also liked seeing how happy she looked. Not only because I wanted her to be happy, which I did, but because seeing her that way took me off the hook. I didn't have to be so worried all the time or trying to figure out ways to cheer her up.

Lunchtime, Frank made another of his amazing soups, out of potatoes and onions this time, that he served cold, which was perfect for a day like that. After, my mother decided to give him a haircut. Then Frank said he thought I should get a haircut and he gave me one. He was surprisingly good at this. At the prison, he said, he cut everyone's hair. They weren't allowed to have scissors, but there was one guy on the cellblock who had a pair that he hid inside a loose piece of cement in the yard.

Frank hardly ever said anything about where he'd spent the last eighteen years, but he told us about how, after one of the guards found the scissors, and they all had to go back to prison buzz cuts, the men used to reminisce about the good old days when Frank cut their hair.

My mother taught him how to dance the Texas two-step, though he couldn't really dance too well yet because of his leg.

As soon as I'm all mended up, Adele, he told her, I'm taking you out on the town.

This would be in Canada.

It was so hot, we weren't hungry for dinner, but my mother made popcorn, with melted butter, and we laid pillows on the floor in front of the TV set and watched a movie, *Tootsie*.

That's what we could do, when we cross the border, my mother said to Frank. Dress you up like a woman. You could wear one of my costumes.

Her saying that brought us back to how things were for us. For one day, we had gotten to act like we were these three carefree people with no troubles bigger than getting the garbage disposal unclogged, but when the picture came to us, of crossing the border into a different country, with a carload of everything we had in the world, from our old lives, and no idea where we were headed except away, a silence came over us.

Trying to break it, maybe, my mother said, Dustin Hoffman looks sort of nice as a woman.

I'm more the Jessica Lange type, I said.

I'm more the Adele type, Frank said.

After the movie was over, I told them I was tired, and headed up the stairs, but not really to bed. I sat for a while at my desk. I was thinking I should write my father a letter. I figured I wouldn't see him for a long time, and even though the times when I did see him were hardly ever good, I still felt sad.

Dear Dad, I wrote. *I can't say where I'm going right now but I don't want you to worry.*

Dear Dad, I started again. *You might not be hearing from me for a while.*

I want you to know, I really appreciate all the times you took me out for dinner.

I want you to know, I appreciate when you helped me with my science project.

I know how hard you worked to bring us all to Disney World.

I'm happy you've got some other kids around, to keep you busy.

I don't blame you for anything.

Sometimes it's a good thing for people not to see each other for a while. When they get back together, they have a lot of things to tell each other.

You don't have to worry about me, I wrote. *I'm going to be fine.*

Say good-bye to Richard and Chloe for me. Also Marjorie.

I had hesitated a long time, when I got to the bottom of the page. I decided on *Sincerely yours.* Then just *Sincerely.* Then I crossed that out. Then I thought about how stupid it would look, having a cross-out, and how, if he looked close, he'd still make out the word I'd written in the first place, and wrote *Yours truly.* Safer than the alternative, which had been *Love.*

Chapter 19

Tuesday morning. School was supposed to start the next day. My mother was cleaning out the refrigerator. She had started boxing things up to take in the car, but there was surprisingly little. Our dishes had come from the Goodwill. A couple of pots and pans, also nothing special. The coffeepot.

We'd take her tape player, but not the television. I had turned it on when I came down, to keep me company while I ate my cereal. Jerry Lewis had signed off, finally, but now we had Regis and Kathie Lee checking in.

I won't miss that sound, my mother said about the TV set. On Prince Edward Island, we can listen to the birds.

You know what we'll do, Henry? she said. We'll get you a violin. We'll find an old Canadian fiddle player to teach you how to play.

She wasn't bringing her cello since it didn't actually belong to her, though considering the other major law we were breaking, by crossing the border with Frank, I wouldn't have thought stealing a rental cello was such a big deal. Never mind, she said. I'll get one up there. Full size this time. We can play together, once you learn your violin.

One thing she felt bad about was abandoning all our supplies—the year's inventory of paper towels and toilet paper, our store of Campbell's soup. Frank said there was no room in the car for those, and anyway, if they stopped us at the border to look through what we had, it would look suspicious. She could bring some of her clothes but not everything. All her wonderful dancing outfits—sparkly skirts and scarves, hats with silk flowers, tap shoes and her soft leather ballet slippers and the high heels she used to wear when she went tango dancing. She'd have to pick out just a few favorites. No room for more.

She had to bring our photograph albums. Almost nothing from her own childhood, but half a dozen leather volumes documenting mine, though in every picture where my father appeared, she had taken a razor blade and cut out his face. In a couple of the pictures where I appeared—at age two, age three, age four—she was wearing a baggy top indicating a pregnancy. Then you turned the page, and no baby. Though in the back of one volume, there was a footprint, no bigger than a stamp. Fern.

In my case, there wasn't all that much I cared about, to pack. My *Chronicles of Narnia* and my *Giant Treasury of Magic Tricks* and, from when I was little, *Pokey Little Puppy* and *Curious George*. My poster of Albert Einstein sticking out his tongue.

When you got down to it, the main thing I cared about was Joe. Except for when we brought him home from the pet store, he'd never ridden in a car before, but I figured I could take him out of his cage if he got scared, and just hold him under my shirt, where he could feel my heart. I liked to do that sometimes, even when we weren't going anyplace. I could feel his too, faster than mine, under his soft silky fur.

He hadn't been doing well in the heat wave. It had been a couple of days since he'd shown any interest in his wheel. He just lay around on the floor of the cage, panting, with a glassy expression. He hadn't touched his food. I had fed him some water with an eyedropper, because the effort required to get up and drink had seemed too much for him.

I'm worried about Joe, I told my mother that morning. I wouldn't want to take him in the car till the weather cools down.

We need to talk about that, Henry, she said. I don't think they allow hamsters to cross the border.

We'll have to smuggle him, I said. I can put him under my shirt. I was already planning to carry him there so he wouldn't be scared.

If they found Joe, they'd start checking everything out. Pretty soon they'd discover about Frank. The police would arrest him. They'd send us back.

He's part of our family. We can't leave him.

We'll find him a good home, she said. Maybe the Jervises would like him for their grandchildren.

I looked at Frank. He was down on the floor, scrubbing the linoleum. They wanted to leave everything looking really nice, my mother had said. She didn't want people talking about her. Now he was holding a knife, running it along the place where the tile met the drywall, to dig out any built-up dirt. He didn't look up, didn't meet my eyes. My mother was rubbing steel wool over the toaster oven, over and over, in the same spot.

If Joe doesn't go, neither do I, I told her. He's the one thing I care about here.

She knew better than to say we'd get another hamster. Or a dog, even though I'd always wanted one.

You never even asked me if I minded not seeing my dad anymore, I said. Some people get to have brothers and sisters. All I have is Joe.

I knew what that would do to her. On the outside, the parts of her face all stayed in the same position, but it was as if someone injected a chemical in her at that moment, with some strange and terrible toxic effect. Like her skin froze.

It could ruin everything, she said. Her voice was so quiet now I could barely hear. You're asking me to put a man I love in jeopardy for a hamster.

I hated how ridiculous she made it sound. Like my whole life was based on a joke.

Only the things you care about are important, I said. You and him. All you want to do is get into bed with him and fuck.

It was not a word I'd ever used before. It was not a word I'd ever heard spoken in our house. Until I heard it coming out of my mouth, I would not have believed a word could possess so much power.

I remembered the time she poured the milk on the floor, and another time—so long ago the memory was like an old Polaroid photograph that's almost faded out—where she had sat in the closet with some kind of cloth over her eyes, with a sound coming out of her like a dying animal. Much later I realized, this must have been after the baby died. The last one. Until this moment, I'd forgotten it, but now I could see her squatting on the floor, with the coats hanging over her, and our winter boots jumbled up on the floor around her, along with an umbrella and the hose of the vacuum cleaner. It was a sound like nothing I'd heard before, and after hearing it I had flung myself on top of her as if I could plug it up. I put my hand over her mouth and rubbed my shirt on her face, but the sound kept coming.

This time, there was no sound. That turned out to be worse. This was how I pictured Hiroshima, which I did a report on once, after they dropped the bomb. Wherever a person was when it happened, they remained frozen there, with the skin melting off their face, and their eyes staring.

My mother stood there. She was still holding the toaster oven. She was barefoot, with a rag in her hand from cleaning out the crumbs. She didn't move.

Frank was the one who spoke. He set down the knife and got up off the floor and wrapped his long arm around her shoulders.

It's all right, Adele, he said. We can work this out. We'll bring the hamster. But Henry, I'm asking you to apologize to your mother.

I went up to my room. I started taking my clothes out of the drawers. T-shirts of sports teams I didn't care about. A baseball cap from a Red Sox game my father took Richard and me to see, where I took out my puzzle book in the seventh inning. A couple of letters from Arak, the African pen pal, who we'd lost track of a couple of years back. A piece of pyrite I had believed, when I was little, to be gold. I had this idea when I got it that someday I'd sell it and make a whole lot of money and take my mother on an amazing trip. Somewhere like New York City or Las Vegas, where they'd have dancing. Not Prince Edward Island.

I went in my mother's room, where the cassette player was. I unplugged the machine and carried it into my room, put in one of my tapes. Guns N' Roses, top volume. It wasn't a very good cassette player, so when you turned it up loud, there was a scratchy sound to the bass line, but that was probably the point.

I stayed in my room all afternoon. Everything I owned I put in trash bags. A couple of times, as I was tossing things in the bags, I'd hesitate and consider saving something, but I wanted this to be slash and burn. Once you started holding things back, it wasn't the same.

Sometime in the late afternoon, when the last of my stuff had been bagged up and carried down the steps and I'd set everything by the trash cans, I got out Eleanor's number. I took my time walking through the living room toward the phone, past my mother and Frank, taking the books off the shelves, putting them

238 • JOYCE MAYNARD

in boxes, to set out by the library for the twenty-five-cent sale where most of them had come from in the first place.

Let them wonder.

I picked up the receiver and dialed. She answered on the first ring.

You want to get together?

Under other circumstances, my mother would have asked where I was going. This time she said nothing, but I told her anyway.

I'm going to see a girl I know, I said. In case you wondered.

My mother turned around and looked at me. The look on her face reminded me of the first time my father had come by to pick me up that time, after Chloe was born, and we were in the yard, and the car window was open, so we could hear her crying. That was when I understood, hitting a person with your fist wasn't the only way to take them out.

We won't do anything you wouldn't do, I said, as the door slammed after me.

I met Eleanor at the playground at the park, but nobody else was there. Too hot. We sat on the swings. She was wearing a dress so short it made you think maybe she hadn't finished getting dressed.

You won't believe what my mother did, I said. She thought we could just leave my hamster behind.

Eleanor was fingering her braid. Now she took the tip of it and drew it across her lips, as if it were a brush and she was painting them.

You might not be familiar with this, but psychologists say that you can tell a lot about someone from how they treat animals. Not that your mother's a bad person or anything. But if you look at psychopathic killers, they nearly always started out by torturing pets. John Wayne Gacy, Charles Manson. You should hear what they did to cats before they got around to people.

I hate them both, I said. Frank and my mother. She doesn't even think about what I might want. Frank pretends to be concerned, but really he just wants to get in good with her.

The sex drug. I told you, Eleanor said.

They think they're in charge of me.

You just figured that out? Parents are always that way. They like us when we're babies, but as soon as we have our own ideas that might be different from what they want, they have to shut us up. Like yesterday, this woman called from the school I want to go to, to talk to my dad about whether there might be a way to set him up on a payment plan. I was listening in.

You want to know what he told her? *Actually, my ex-wife and I have decided the best thing for Eleanor at this point is to have her living with a family member. She's been having issues with an eating disorder, which made us conclude we could monitor her best from home.*

Like he was only thinking about me. Like it had nothing to do with the twelve thousand dollars he didn't want to come up with, she said.

My mother never even talked to my father about taking me away, I said. She never discussed it with me.

The truth was, one part about the Maritime Province plan that sounded good to me was not having to go out anymore for those Saturday nights at Friendly's with my father and Marjorie. But my mother shouldn't have assumed it. She should have consulted me.

Parents have to be the boss of everything, Eleanor said. Once you report this guy and they take him away, that's really going to stick it to her. You having the power for a change.

Up until then, all I knew was how mad I felt—mad, and a whole lot of other feelings, none of them good. First I was scared that my mother and Frank might be leaving me. Then I felt sort of left out, that I wasn't the most important person in my mother's world anymore, and scared, that I didn't know what would happen. But however I was feeling—even upset as I was—I knew I didn't want to stick it to my mother.

I wanted her to be happy, actually. I just wished she'd be happy with me.

The other part of what Eleanor had said—the part about seeing to it that Frank got taken away—almost made me shiver. I didn't want to, but I was thinking about playing catch with him. I was thinking about the two of us in the kitchen, the blueberry pancake he made for my mother in the shape of a heart, the way he'd lifted Barry out of the tub that time, and sat him down on the bed after, to cut his fingernails. How he had whistled while he washed the dishes. Saying, *The richest man in America isn't eating a pie as good as we are, tonight.* Saying, *See the ball, Henry?*

I've been thinking some more about that idea you had, I said. Even though they did all this stuff, I don't think I can do something that would send him back to prison. He'd probably have to stay there a long time, if they captured him now. They'd punish him even worse for escaping.

That's the point, Henry. Remove him, remember? Get him out of your life, Eleanor said.

But he might not deserve to rot in jail forever either, I said. He's sort of a nice guy, except for wanting to take my mom away. And if he went back to prison, my mother would be really sad. She might not get over it.

For a while she'd be sad, Eleanor said. Eventually she'd thank you for it. And don't forget the money.

I'm just a kid, I told her. I don't really need that much money.

Are you joking? she said. You know all the things you could do with that reward? You could buy a car and have it ready for when you get your license. You could buy all this great stereo equipment. You could go to New York City and stay in a hotel. You could even apply to the Weathervane School like I did. I bet you'd love it there.

It just doesn't seem fair. It's like being a tattletale. They shouldn't reward people for doing that kind of thing.

Eleanor tossed her head to get her bangs out of her face and looked at me with her unnaturally large eyes—the only eyes I'd ever seen on a person where you could see the whites all around the iris part, which gave her charisma, but also had the effect of making her look a little like a cartoon character. She reached out a hand and touched my cheek. Stroked my neck. She moved her hand down the front of my shirt, like something she might have seen someone do in a movie. I hadn't noticed this before, but her fingernails were bitten so low, you could actually see blood on the tips.

She said, One thing I love about you, Henry, is how kind you are. Even to people who may not deserve it. You're actually tons more sensitive than most girls I know.

I just don't want anyone to get hurt, I said. I had gotten up off the swing now and walked over to a patch of grass and sat down. She followed me. She grabbed my shoulders and whirled me around so our faces were close enough that I could feel her breath on me.

She kissed me then. Only this time, as it had been in the scene I had dreamed up, I was lying down, not standing up. She was on top of me, with her tongue in my mouth again, but deeper this time, and her other hand moving down my chest, and lower.

Look what happened, she said. I made you get an erection.

This was the way she talked. She could say any-thing.

We could have sex, she said. I never actually did it before but we have this interesting chemical attraction going on.

She was pulling off her underpants. Purple, with red hearts.

All this time that I'd been thinking about doing it, with no real prospect, and now here it was, but I couldn't. Nobody was around. But it didn't feel safe.

I think we should know each other better first, I said. I hated it that when I spoke, instead of my new low voice coming out, it was my old one from sixth grade, the higher one.

If you're worried about me getting pregnant you don't need to, she said. I haven't had my period in months. That means there aren't any prime eggs hanging around inside me at the moment.

She had her hand on my penis now. She was holding on, as if she was some movie star who had just won an Oscar. Or some local broadcaster on the scene at a car wreck and this was the microphone. That, more so.

You know what will happen if you don't report him to the police? she said. They'll take you away and we won't ever get to see each other anymore. And I'll be stuck back at Holton Mills Junior High with no friends. I might stop eating entirely, in which case they'd probably send me back to the eating disorder clinic.

I can't, I told her. I'm too young. I couldn't believe I said that.

I think my mother and Frank are trying to do the best they can, I told her. It's not their fault.

You are unreal, she said, standing up and stepping back into her underwear, with those skinny legs of hers that made me think of a chicken wing.

I always knew you were a dork, she said, but I was thinking you had potential. Now it turns out you're just an idiot.

She had put her dress on. She was standing over me now, brushing the dust off her chest and braiding her hair, from where it had gotten messed up.

I can't believe I used to think you were cool, she said. You were right all the time. You told me you were a total loser.

That night, my mother served us Cap'n Andy's. There were so many fish dinners left, it seemed like a good idea to use up a few.

We sat around the table without talking. My mother had poured herself a glass of wine, and then another, but Frank wasn't drinking anything. Partway through the meal, I got up and went into the living room. A bunch of actors dressed as raisins were dancing around a giant cereal bowl.

Frank and my mother had mostly packed the car up. The plan was to take off in the morning, after a stop at the bank. One question was how much cash my mother could withdraw, without attracting suspicion. They could use every dollar, but taking that much might be risky, though once they left, it might be impossible to get any more money out of her account.

Trying to get it from Canada would tip the authorities off.

I wasn't tired, but I went upstairs early. My room was mostly bare now. Nothing but an old *Star Wars* poster on the wall and a certificate from two years ago that said I participated in Little League. Even the clothes we weren't taking with us, which was most of them, had been boxed up and left next to the Goodwill collection bin. My mother said she didn't want strangers pawing through our stuff after we were gone. Better to give it away where nobody would know where it came from.

I tried to read but I couldn't. I was thinking about Eleanor, the sight of her thin brown legs, kneeling over me, and her sharp ribs, her bony elbows pressing down on my chest. I tried putting some different pictures in my head instead—of Olivia Newton-John or the girl from *The Dukes of Hazzard,* or Jill from *Charlie's Angels,* the sister from *Happy Days,* even. Friendlier types of girls, but I couldn't stop seeing her face, hearing the sound of her voice.

I made you get an erection.
Dork. Idiot. Loser.

Sometime later, I heard the sound of my mother and Frank coming up the stairs. The other nights, I'd heard them whispering, and sometimes muffled laughter. She would brush her hair, or he'd brush it for her. Then the shower. Water. I couldn't hear this, but I imagined hands on skin, and one time I had heard a slapping sound, followed by more laughter.

Stop that.

You know you like it.

Yes.

That night, no sounds came from her bedroom. I could hear them climbing into bed, the creak of the springs as they lowered their bodies on the mattress, then nothing. No headboard. No moaning. No bird cries.

I lay there waiting for murmurs of love to come through the wall, but there was nothing. I held my breath, but all I heard was the sound of my own heart beating. I missed the sound of their voices.

Adele. Adele. Adele.

Frank. Frank.

Adele.

The window was open, but the last of the weekend barbecues and neighborhood parties were over. No ball game; the Red Sox must be off. Up and down the street, the lights in every house were out. No light but the fluorescent blue of the Edwardses' bug zapper and the faint sizzling sound when a mosquito hit the grid.

Chapter 20

Wednesday. There was no coffee that morning. My mother had packed the pot. No eggs on the stove either. We'll stop on the road, she said. Once we got out on the highway.

It was one of those moments again where for just a second you forget what's going on, when you first open your eyes. Waking up in my room with everything gone, it took me a second to know where I was, even. Then I did.

We're leaving, I said. I wasn't talking to anyone. I just wanted to hear the words. The sound of my voice was different, in an empty room, with the rug rolled up and my stuff gone. On my desk was the envelope with the note for my father, that I stuck in my pocket. Otherwise, nothing.

It was raining, the sky a dull inky gray. I thought about the boxes of books and clothes we'd left outside next to the Goodwill shed last night. They'd be no good now. But it was a relief that the heat had finally broken.

Someone was in the shower. Frank, from the sound of it, because I heard whistling. I went downstairs. It was still very early, six o'clock maybe, but I could hear my mother moving around.

She was standing in the door to the mudroom. She had on a pair of checkered pants she'd had for as long as I could remember. I realized how thin she'd gotten lately.

I have some bad news.

I looked at her. I tried to imagine what my mother would consider bad news. Not the same things as normal people.

It's Joe, she said. When I went to carry his cage out to the car, he wasn't moving. He was just lying there.

I ran to the mudroom.

He's just tired, I told her. He doesn't like to run around a lot when it's hot. He was nibbling around in my hand last night when I picked him up to say good night.

He was lying on the newspaper. His eyes were open, but they were staring, and his paws were stretched

250 · JOYCE MAYNARD

out in front of him like a superhero in the flying position. His tail was curled under him, and his mouth was
slightly open, as if he'd wanted to say something.

You killed him, I said. The two of you. You never
wanted Joe to come with us, so you figured you'd get
rid of him.

You don't believe that, she said. You know I'd never
do anything like that. Neither would Frank.

Oh yeah? If I recall correctly, he let his own kid die.

Out in the yard it was still mostly dark. The rain made
it hard to get my shovel in the earth. The ground was
heavy with mud.

While I was digging the grave for Joe, I reconsid-
ered my decision not to call the police. I didn't care
about getting the stuff in the SkyMall catalog anymore.
I just wanted to punish the two of them. Reporting
Frank to the police would do that all right.

I swear to you, my mother said. She had followed me
out to the yard. I would never hurt anything you loved.

I started digging. I thought about the story she'd
told me that time, when I was young, and she explained
why I was an only child. I pictured her out in the yard
at our old house, my father's house, digging a hole
with a trowel, laying in the ground the blood clot,
wrapped in a cloth handkerchief, that was going to be

my brother or sister. And the other time: the cigar box with Fern's ashes inside.

Frank was there too now, only when he started to come closer, my mother pushed him back.

Henry might just want to be alone, she said.

At first, when I set out down the street, I didn't know where I was going, but I kept walking a long time. Partway there, I realized I was headed to my father's house.

Standing outside in the yard, I could see a light in one of the upstairs windows. My father would be up already, sitting in the kitchen alone with his coffee, reading the sports page. Marjorie would come down in a minute to heat the water for Chloe's bottle, that she still liked first thing when she got up.

My father would kiss his wife on the cheek. He'd look up from the paper to say something about the rain. Nothing special, but it would be nice in the kitchen. It was only times like going to Friendly's or trying to get Richard and me into a conversation about our favorite player on the Sox when things didn't work very well. Except for me, they were a regular family.

On my way over, I had considered going to the door when I got there. I had pictured myself telling him, You know how you always said my mother was crazy? Well, listen to this.

They would have me moved in by dinnertime. My bag was even packed already. I'd have to share a room with Richard, which he'd hate. They'd probably get us bunk beds.

I wondered if he engaged in some of the same nighttime activities I did. The only person who would give him a hard-on was Jose Canseco, probably. I couldn't picture the two of us discussing it. Marjorie, when she did the laundry, would tell my father, You need to have a talk with your son.

In the past, I used to be mad at my father all the time, but standing in the rain that morning, watching his shadow pass across the window, listening to the back door slam when he let out their cat, hearing the voice of Chloe—I never called her my sister, or my half sister, knowing how my mother would feel if I did— calling out for one of them to get her out of the crib, all I felt was sadness. This place was their home. It wasn't mine. It wasn't anybody's fault. Just how things happened.

I left the envelope with my letter in their mailbox. I knew his routine. He picked up the mail as he pulled in the driveway, coming home from work. Sometime around dinnertime he'd read it. By then I'd be someplace around the Canadian border.

As I walked home, a police car pulled over. It was still very early, and I was wet from not having a raincoat on. The rain had gotten heavier. My pants were so wet they were dragging in puddles, and my shirt stuck to me. Water ran down my face, making it hard to see.

You need some help, son? The policeman had rolled down his window.

I'm OK.

You want to tell me where you're going? he said. It's pretty early for someone your age to be out on the road without a jacket or anything. Isn't this the first day of school for you?

I was just taking a walk, I said. I'm heading back home now.

Hop in. I'll drive you. Your parents are probably worried about you, he said.

Just my mother, I told him. But she won't be.

Just to be on the safe side, I'm going to have a word with your mom. I've got a boy about your age.

We passed the Pricemart and the library, and my school, where a few cars were in the parking lot. Eager-beaver-type teachers, putting the last touches on their classrooms, only I wasn't going to be there.

We passed the bank. Turned right up the hill, left onto my street. Past the Edwardses and the Jervises, all the way to the end. Mad as I was at my mother, I was sending her brain waves to not be out at the curb, packing boxes in the car. Most of all, I didn't want

Frank to be there. I was transmitting a message to him the way Silver Surfer did, with his telepathic powers, to go back in the house, upstairs, out of sight.

She was outside in her checkered pants with a rain poncho on, but no boxes, which was good. When she saw the police car stop in front of the house, she put a hand over her eyes, but that could have been to just keep the rain out, it was falling so hard now.

Mrs. Johnson, he said. I found your boy here out by the highway. I thought I'd bring him home to you. Particularly considering the fact he's supposed to be in school in around forty-five minutes. Also he's soaking wet.

She just stood there. I had seen what happened to her hands, just from going through the checkout line at the store, so I could imagine how they were trembling now. She kept them in her pocket.

What grade are you anyway? he said. I'm guessing sixth? Maybe you know my son.

Seventh, I told him.

Gotcha. I guess that would mean you'll be a lot more interested in the girls than some pipsqueak sixth grader, right, Henry?

Thank you for bringing him home, my mother said. She was looking back to the house. I knew what she was thinking.

Any time, he said. He looks like a good kid. Just keep him that way. He extended his hand, to shake hers. I knew why she didn't take her hands out of her pockets. I shook his hand myself, just so he wouldn't wonder.

The night before, on our way to drop stuff off at the Goodwill box—our third run—we stopped by the house where Evelyn and Barry lived. My mother wanted to give some of my old toys to Barry. There was a Rubik's cube and an Etch-A-Sketch that I didn't think he'd have much use for, and a Magic Eight ball where, when you picked it up, there was a message on the bottom showing through a little plastic window— something meant to tell you what you should do with your life. I didn't know how useful that would be for Barry, but my mother thought he might like to have some things for his room to make it look like a place a regular kid lived in. I was giving him my lava lamp too, though I didn't want to. My mother said that was just the kind of thing that could get us in trouble if we tried taking it across the border. They'd think we were into drugs.

Evelyn was wearing a workout suit when she came to the door. She must have been working out to her Richard Simmons tape. She always said *we* when she talked about the things she did, as if Barry did them too, but really he just sat in his chair waving his arms to the music and making noises. Johnny Cash was definitely his favorite, but he liked Richard Simmons too.

Now, when he saw us, he started making noises, like he was excited. He was facing the TV screen, where a bunch of women in sweatbands were doing jumping jacks, and he was bouncing in his chair, but when he saw me, he started pointing at the screen, and pointing at me and yelling, only this time I understood what he was saying, even if nobody else did. He was saying *Frank*. He wanted to know where Frank was.

Back home, I told him. No harm in telling him. I knew his mother wouldn't understand. One person that was definitely not going to pick up the phone and collect any ten thousand dollars was Barry.

My mother had not explained to Evelyn that we were leaving. All she said was that I'd been cleaning out my room. Back to school and all.

I wish I could have told her good-bye, my mother said, as we drove home. Maybe she wasn't the greatest friend a person could have, but she was the only one I had. I guess I'll never see her again.

Only we did. Shortly after the police officer had dropped me off, there was Evelyn, knocking at the door.

This time Frank was in the living room when she showed up. He turned around so only his back was visible, like he was fixing a light or something, but it had to seem pretty obvious that we were moving out. There was also no good way of concealing the fact that we had a man in our house.

Oh gosh, Evelyn said. It looks like I came over at a bad time. I just wanted to show you my appreciation for helping out with Barry the other day, Adele. You were a lifesaver.

She had made cinnamon rolls—though having sampled her baking in the past, I wasn't getting my hopes up. My mother used to say Evelyn was the only person she knew who could mess up a Pillsbury slice-and-bake roll. Of course, Evelyn was also just about the only person my mother knew, period.

I guess I might be interrupting something, she said. I didn't know you had company.

From behind her, on the step, Barry was making wild hooting noises, like some kind of jungle bird, and flailing. I knew from experience now that the word he was saying was Frank's name. Though Frank was keeping his back to us.

I'm sorry I don't have time to introduce you, my mother said. This gentleman here was just fixing something for us. Henry and I are taking a trip.

Evelyn peered into the living room. The rug was gone. Also all our books, and my mother's framed print of a painting of a mother with a child on her lap, and the museum poster we always had up of a goldfish in a bowl, and one of a couple of ballerinas practicing. Through the door to the kitchen, you could see the shelves were empty of dishes.

I see, said Evelyn. She didn't ask where we were headed on this trip of ours, as if she already understood she wasn't going to get the real story.

So, thanks again for the rolls, my mother said. They look wonderful.

Maybe I should get my plate back now, Evelyn said. In case you're gone for a long time.

There was no longer any plate of our own to put them on, so my mother set the rolls on the morning paper, its headline plainly visible. In the wake of last week's prison escape, the governor was announcing tightened security measures being instituted at the prison. Just to remind everyone who might have missed the original story, they were once again running the photograph of Frank, with the numbers across his chest.

Take care of yourself, Evelyn, my mother told her.

You too.

We were at the bank at 9:00 A.M. when the doors opened. Just my mother and me. Frank had stayed home. The plan was that once we had the money, we'd swing on back to the house and pick him up before hitting the road, north toward the border.

In the past when we needed cash, I was the one who went in to get it, leaving my mother in the car. The amounts I withdrew were never all that much, and the tellers knew me. This time my mother said she figured she'd have to go in herself, since she was cleaning out her account. As close as she dared.

She was holding her passbook, and she had put on an outfit that she must have thought looked like something a person might wear if they were withdrawing eleven thousand three hundred dollars from their savings account. I stood next to her. There were two people in the line ahead of us. One an old woman, with a lot of coins to cash in. And a man depositing a couple of checks.

Then it was our turn. My mother's hands were shaking as she set the passbook on the counter, along with the withdrawal slip.

I would have thought you'd be in school today, son, the teller said. From her name tag I knew her name was Muriel.

My son's got a dentist appointment, my mother said. I knew this sounded ridiculous. Even a person like my mother would never schedule an appointment on the first day of school.

That's why we need this money, actually, she said. Braces.

Goodness, that's some expensive dental work, Muriel said. If you haven't committed yet, you might want to try my daughter's orthodontist. He's got us on a payment plan.

It's dental, plus other things, my mother said. An appendectomy.

I looked at her. That must have been the only kind of surgery she could come up with, but of all the choices she might have mentioned, this was the dumbest.

I'll be right back, Muriel told us. With an amount this large, I just need to get it approved by my supervisor. Not that there will be any problem of course. We know you. We know your son.

A woman came in the bank with a baby in a front-pack. I looked over at my mother. These were sometimes difficult moments for her, but for once she seemed not even to notice.

I shouldn't have tried to get so much, she whispered. I should have only asked for half.

It's going to be OK, I told her. This is probably just standard procedure.

When Muriel came back, there was a man with her.

There's no problem, of course, he said. I just wanted to make sure you aren't experiencing any problems here. It's a somewhat unusual situation, having a person withdraw this much in cash. Normally, when transferring funds of this quantity, our clients prefer to receive a cashier's check.

It just seemed handier, my mother said. Hands in the pockets of her jacket. You know how these days they're always asking for all these forms of identification. It can waste so much time.

Well, then, the supervisor said to Muriel. Let's not keep our friends here waiting.

He scribbled something on a piece of paper. Muriel opened a drawer and started counting out bills. The hundreds came in stacks of ten, tied together. She counted these out too, while my mother studied the stack.

When Muriel had all the bills counted, she asked if my mother had something to put them in. We hadn't thought about that part.

Out in the car, she said. She came back with the bag of hamster food I'd put in the night before. Before putting the money in the bag, she dumped out the last of the dry kibble into the receptacle next to the place where people filled out their deposit and withdrawal slips.

Muriel looked startled. I could give you a few of our zippered money pouches, she said. Would you like a few of those instead?

Actually, this is good, my mother said. If someone ever held us up at gunpoint, they'd never guess we had all this money in with the pet food.

Luckily, we don't have too many criminals around here, right, Adele? Muriel said. She had learned my mother's name from the slip she had filled out with the details of her transaction. It was probably something they taught them in bank teller school: to use people's real name when doing business with them.

Except for that man who escaped last week, she added. Can you believe they still haven't caught him? But I bet he's long gone now.

When we got home, there was a light flashing on the message machine. Frank was standing just inside the doorway.

I didn't pick up the call, Frank said. But I heard the message. Henry's father got wind that you were leaving town with him. He said he was coming over. We'd better get out of here.

I ran upstairs. I had wanted to walk through the rooms slowly, one more time, but now we had to go fast. My father was probably on his way over right now.

Henry, my mother called to me. You have to come now. We have to leave.

I looked out the window one more time, down the street across the roofs of the houses. *Good-bye, tree. Good-bye, yard.*

Now, Henry. I mean it.

Listen to your mother, son. We need to go.

Then we heard a siren coming. Another siren. The sound of car wheels making a fast turn. Our street.

I came back down the stairs. Slower now. Nobody was going anywhere. I knew that now. Overhead, the sound of a helicopter.

My whole life up to then—with the exception of what had taken place with Eleanor—things happened way too slowly, but now it was like we were in a movie, only someone turned it to fast-forward, so it was hard keeping track of the action. Except for my mother. She couldn't move.

She stood now in the almost-empty living room, holding on to the bag of hamster food. Frank stood next to her, like a man about to face the firing squad. He was holding her hand.

It's all right, Adele. Don't be scared.

I don't understand, she said. How did they find out?

My heart was exploding.

I just wrote Dad a letter so he'd know we went away, I said. I didn't mention a single thing about

Frank. I didn't think he'd pick up the letter so early. Normally he never gets the mail till dinnertime.

Outside, the sound of brakes screeching to a stop. One of the cars had pulled up on our lawn, the place my mother had tried to start a wildflower garden, only they didn't come up. A couple of the neighbors who didn't work—Mrs. Jervis, Mr. Temple—had come out on their front steps to see what was going on.

There was a voice on a bullhorn now. *Frank Chambers. We know you're in there. Come out with your hands up and no one will get hurt.*

He stood there with his back very straight, facing the door. Except for that muscle in his neck I'd noticed the day I met him, that had twitched very slightly then too, he could have been one of those people you see in parks sometimes, who dress up and take a pose as if they're a statue, and people put money in their suitcase. That still. Nothing moving but his eyes.

My mother had wrapped her arms around him. Her hands were on his neck, his chest, his hair. She was moving her fingers over the skin of his face as if he were clay and she was sculpting it. Her fingers on his lips, his eyelids. I can't let them take you away, she said. Her voice a whisper.

Listen, Adele, he said. I want you to do everything I say here. We don't have time to discuss this.

There was a piece of rope on the counter that they'd used for tying up the boxes they packed, the things we were supposed to take with us for our new life in Canada. There was a knife left in the drawer, to cut the rope.

Sit in that chair, he told her. His voice was different now. Barely recognizable. Put your hands behind your back. Your feet in front of you. You too, Henry.

He wound the first piece of rope around her right wrist. As he tied, I could see her hand shaking. She was crying now, but he didn't look at her face. He was concentrating on one thing, the knot. When he had formed it, he made a quick, firm tug, tight enough you could see it pulling at the skin on her hand. Any other time, if he'd hurt her in any way, he would have rubbed his finger over the place, but he seemed not to notice, or if he did, to care.

He moved on then to her other hand. Then her feet. To tie those properly, he had to take her shoes off. There was the red polish on her toes. The place, on her ankle, I'd seen him kissing her one time.

We could hear a police radio outside, men on walkie-talkies, the helicopter directly overhead. *Three minutes,* the voice said on the bullhorn. *Come out with your hands up.*

Sit, Henry, Frank said.

The way he said it, you would never know we'd played catch. Never know this was a person who had sat on the step with me once, teaching me a card trick. He was winding the rope around my chest now. No time for individual knots, just one tight loop around my middle, yanked hard enough to force the air out of me. Still, it was just a single knot he made, a single knot he had time for. This would come out later, when some reporter had raised the question we knew was coming, as to whether my mother had been cooperating with Frank. Consider how inadequate the restraints had been on her son, someone had observed. And how, when the two of them went to the bank—victims? perpetrators?—Frank wasn't even with them.

She took that money out of her own free will, they said. Didn't this prove the woman was involved?

But he'd tied her up. There was that. And me too, in a fashion.

More vehicles were screeching down our road. That voice on the bullhorn again. *We don't want to have to use the tear gas.* No time for anything now. *This is your last chance to exit the building peacefully, Chambers,* the voice called out. By then, Frank was already heading to the door. One foot in front of the other. He did not look back.

As instructed, he had his hands above his head. He was still limping from the injury, but he moved with steady deliberation out the door, down the steps, to the lawn where they were waiting for him with the handcuffs.

We couldn't see what happened after that, though soon after, a couple of police officers burst in the door and untied us. A woman officer gave my mother a glass of water and told her there was an ambulance waiting. The woman told my mother she was probably in shock, even if she didn't know it.

Don't be scared, sonny, one of the men told me. Your mom's OK. We've got the guy in custody now. He won't be able to do anything to you and your mom anymore.

My mother was sitting in her chair, still, with her shoes off. She was rubbing her wrists, as if she missed the rope. Where did freedom get you when you thought about it?

Rain was still coming down, though less heavily than before. Just a gentle drizzle. Across the street, I saw Mrs. Jervis taking photographs, and Mr. Temple being interviewed by a reporter. The helicopter had landed in the flat space in the back of our yard, where Frank and I had played catch, the place he had talked about for our Rhode Island Reds, and where, as of this morning, the body of Joe the hamster lay buried.

I knew something was up, Mr. Jervis was saying. When I brought her peaches the other day, I thought she was trying to say something to me in code. But he must have had the eagle eye on her the whole time.

A maroon minivan pulled up. My father. When he saw me, he came running over. What the heck is going on here? he said to one of the policemen. I just thought my ex-wife was losing it. I wasn't expecting to see all you guys here.

Someone called in a tip, the police officer told him.

They were putting Frank in the backseat of one of the police cars now. He had his hands behind his back, and his head was bent down, avoiding the cameras probably. Just before they had him all the way in the car, he looked up one more time, at my mother.

I don't think anyone else saw it but I did. No sound—he was just mouthing the word. *Adele.*

Chapter 21

They charged him with kidnapping my mother and me. This time, they'd lock him up and throw away the key, they said.

When she heard this, my mother—a woman who hardly ever drove anyplace anymore—drove to the capital to see the prosecutor, with me alongside to be her witness. She had to make him understand, she told him, that no unlawful detainment was involved here. Of her own free will, she had invited Frank into our home. He was good to her son. He took care of her. They were going to get married, somewhere in the Maritime Provinces. They were in love.

This prosecutor was a hard-liner, recently elected to office to support the governor's war on crime. The question will have to be considered, he told her, why your son never reported what was going on. They'd take my age into account, he said, but it was possible—unlikely perhaps, but possible—that I'd be viewed as an accomplice to a felony. This wouldn't be the first time that a thirteen-year-old served time in juvenile detention, though probably only for a year. Two at most.

My mother, on the other hand, could be looking at a significantly stiffer sentence. Harboring a fugitive, contributing to the delinquency of a minor. She would lose custody of me, naturally. They were already speaking to my father about that. Evidently even before this episode, there had been incidents suggesting questionable judgment on the part of my mother.

For once, my mother said nothing, driving home. That night, we ate our soup in silence, out of two bowls retrieved from the backseat of our car. Over the next few days, anytime we needed a cup or a plate, a spoon, a towel, that's what we did. Go out to the car for it.

School was in session now. I entered seventh grade enjoying a new and unexpected fame that translated into something like popularity. Is it true, a guy asked me, in gym—as the two of us exited the shower, naked and dripping—that he tortured you? Was your mother his sex slave?

With girls, my recent adventures seemed to translate into something resembling sex appeal. Rachel McCann—for years, the chief object of my fantasies—

found me at my locker one day as I was gathering my books to make a hasty retreat home.

I just wanted you to know I think you're incredibly brave, she said. If you ever want to talk about it, I'm here for you.

It was one of the many regrettable aspects of that strange holiday weekend that just at the moment when I had finally won the notice of the girl I'd dreamed about since second grade, all I wanted was to be left alone. For the first time, I understood my mother's decision, years ago, to simply stay home. Though for me, this was not an option.

Around this time, my mother discontinued her subscription to the newspaper, though I followed the case by reading the paper at the library. If she ever fully understood how it had happened that charges were never pressed against her, that there was never a trial, she didn't talk about it and I didn't bring it up. Had the D.A. chosen to pursue the matter, it would not have been difficult to extract testimony from Evelyn (as for Barry, nobody thought about what he might have to offer) in which it would have been apparent that over the six days in question, my mother had not appeared to be under duress, or doing anything—besides taking care of Evelyn's son, perhaps—she didn't want to do.

But I understood, more than you might think a thirteen-year-old would. Frank had struck a deal. Full confession. Waiving right to trial. In exchange for the assurance that they'd leave my mother and me out of it. Which they did.

They gave Frank ten years for the escape, and fifteen for the attempted kidnapping. It's ironic, the prosecutor said, when you consider that this man would have been up for parole in eighteen months. But we're talking about a violent criminal here. A man without control over his own crazed mind.

I can't regret anything, Frank told my mother, in the only letter she received from him, after the sentencing. If I'd never jumped out that window, I never would have found you.

Given his escape attempt, Frank was designated a high-risk prisoner, requiring detention in a maximum-security facility of a kind that did not exist in our state, or anywhere close. They sent him briefly to upstate New York, where my mother tried to visit him one time. She drove all the way, but when she got there, they told her he was doing solitary. Sometime after that, they transferred him to someplace in Idaho.

For a while, after it happened, my mother's hands shook so violently she couldn't even open a can of

Campbell's soup. She voluntarily relinquished custody of me to my father. Right before he came to pick me up, to take me over to the house where I would live with him and Marjorie and the munchkins, I told her I would never forgive her, but I did. She could have pointed out things I had done, far worse, but she forgave me those.

So I moved into my father's house, the one he shared with Marjorie. As I'd anticipated, they bought a bunk bed so Richard and I could more easily share his small room. He took the bottom bunk.

Lying on the top, at night, I no longer touched myself as I had back home. As much as I had loved that new and mysterious sensation, I associated it now with everything that broke a person's heart: whispering and kisses in the dark, the slow deep sighs, that animal cry I had only briefly misunderstood as being about pain. Frank's wild, joyful moaning, as if nothing less than the earth itself had opened up and a flood of light obliterated everything.

It all began with bodies touching other bodies, hands on skin. And so I kept mine to my sides, and my breathing steady, and stared up at the ceiling above my hard, narrow pallet, at the face of Albert Einstein, sticking out his tongue. The smartest man who ever lived, maybe. He should know, the whole thing was one big joke.

The only banging audible now, on the other side of the wall, took place around five thirty every morning, the sound of my little sister, Chloe (because that's who she was, I saw now—my sister), announcing to the world that another day had begun. Come get me was her cry, though not in so many words. And so after a while, I did.

Marjorie tried her best. It wasn't her fault I wasn't her son. I stood for everything that wasn't normal in the very normal life she and my father had set out to make for themselves and her two children. She didn't like me very much, but I didn't like her either. Fair enough.

With Richard, things went better than you might have expected. Whatever our differences—my preference to live in Narnia; his, to play for the Red Sox—there was this one thing we shared. We had, each of us, another parent living in a house away from this one—somebody whose blood ran in our veins. Whatever his real father's story was, I didn't know it, but thirteen wasn't too young to understand that sorrow and regret took many forms.

No doubt Richard's father, like my mother, had once held his infant son in his arms, looked into the eyes of his child's mother, and believed they would move into the future together with love. The fact that they didn't was a weight each of us carried, as every child does, probably, whose parents no longer live under the same roof. Wherever it is you make your home, there is always this other place, this other person, calling to you. Come to me. Come back.

With my father, those first few weeks after I moved back into our old house, I got the feeling he didn't know what to say to me, and so, more often than not, he said nothing. I knew that papers had been filed, statements made to the court, concerning my mother's questionable parenting choices, as revealed by recent events, but to his credit he didn't say a word about any of that to me. The newspapers had said it all anyway.

A few weeks after I moved in with my father and Marjorie—around the time I chose not to try out for either lacrosse or soccer—my father brought up the idea of taking a bike ride together. In some households—I can't say *families*, because I didn't consider us to be one—this might not have seemed like such a big deal, except that in the past, he'd never seemed to acknowledge the existence of any athletic activity in which no score was involved, no trophies awarded, no winners or losers identified.

When I reminded him my bike had been out of commission for almost two years, he suggested it was time to buy me a new one—a mountain bike, twenty-one speeds. And a bike for himself. That weekend, the two of us drove to Vermont—this being the time of year when fall foliage was particularly great—and rode through a bunch of towns together, staying in a motel outside of Saxons River. One good thing about riding a bicycle: you don't do all that much talking when you're riding one. Especially on those long Vermont hills.

That night, though, we went out to a diner where they had a prime rib special. For most of the meal, we sat in near silence. But around the time the waitress brought his coffee, something seemed to change in my father. Who he seemed like, in a funny way, was Frank, back at my mother's house, as the police cars were closing in, with the helicopter overhead, the bullhorns blaring. He was like a man who knew he was running out of time, and it was now or never. A little like Frank, he surrendered then.

What he did actually was he got on a subject we had generally avoided up until then, my mother. Not the part about her not getting a real job, for once, or whether she was mentally stable enough to take care of me, perhaps because from the looks of things it had already been established, she wasn't. It was their early days together that he spoke of.

You know she was a terrific woman, he said. Funny. Beautiful. You never saw anyone dance like her, north of the Broadway stage.

I just sat there, eating my rice pudding. Picking out the raisins, actually. I didn't look at him, but I was listening.

That trip we made to California was one of the best times I ever had, he told me. We had so little money, we slept in the car, mostly. But there was this one town we passed through, in Nebraska, where we got a motel room with a kitchenette, and we made spaghetti on the hot plate. We didn't know a thing about Hollywood was the truth. We were small-town people. But back in her waitress days she'd waited on a woman one time who was one of the June Taylor dancers on Jackie Gleason, who had written down her number and told Adele to look her up if she was ever in L.A. That's what we were going to do: call the June Taylor dancer. Only when we did that, her son answered the phone. She was in a nursing home by then. Senile, basically. You know what your mother did? We went to visit her. She brought cookies.

I did look up from my bowl then. When I did, his face looked different. I had never thought I looked anything like him—had even wondered, once (in fact, this was a topic of speculation raised by Eleanor), if he was really my father at all, we seemed so different from each other. And he, such an unlikely person to have married my mother. But looking across the diner booth now at this pale, slightly overweight man with his thinning hair and the newly purchased spandex bicycle shirt he'd probably never wear again, I recognized, weirdly, something familiar. I could imagine him being young. I imagined him as that young man my mother had described, who knew just how much pressure to apply to a woman's back as he moved her across the dance floor, the crazy young man she had trusted to keep her from falling when she executed her three-hundred-and-sixty-degree flip in her red underwear. I could see my own face in his, actually. He wasn't crying, but his eyes looked moist.

It was losing those babies that did her in, he said. The last one. She never could get over that.

There was still pudding in my bowl, but I had stopped eating now. My father hadn't touched his coffee either.

A better man might have stayed around to help her through it, he said. But after a while, I couldn't handle all that sadness. I wanted a regular life. I cut out, basically.

And then Marjorie and I had Chloe. It wasn't as if doing that erased what happened before, but it was easier for me, not to think about it. Where for your mother, the story never went away.

This was as much as he said about it, and we didn't revisit the topic again. He paid the bill, and we went back to our motel room. The next morning we rode a little more, but I was realizing by then how totally unnatural a thing it was for my father to be moving along the hills of Vermont by any means other than a minivan. After a couple of hours, when I suggested we call it a day, he didn't argue. On the way home, I slept, mostly.

I stayed at my father's house for most of that seventh-grade year. One good thing: because I was living with my father and Marjorie, there seemed no need to continue our excruciating tradition of Saturday night dinners at Friendly's. Meals at the house were easier. The television set stayed on, for one thing.

You might have thought my mother would have lobbied hard for visits, but the opposite happened, for a while anyway. She seemed to discourage my coming over, and when I stopped by on the new bike (delivering groceries, and library books, and myself), she would seem busy and distracted.

She had calls to make, she said. Vitamin customers. There were all these chores to be done. She was vague about what the chores could be in a house with no furniture to dust or rugs to vacuum, where no cooking happened, no visitors came by.

She was reading a lot, she said, and it was true. There were books piled up the way the Campbell's soup used to be. Books about unlikely topics: forestry and animal husbandry, chickens, wildflowers, raised-bed gardening, though our yard remained as bare as ever. Her favorite book, which seemed to be on the kitchen table every time I came by, was one volume, published in the fifties, by a couple named Helen and Scott Nearing, called *Living the Good Life*—about their experiences, leaving their jobs and home in some-place like Connecticut and moving to rural Maine, where they had grown all their own food and lived without electricity or telephone. In the photographs il-lustrating the book, Scott Nearing was always pictured wearing overalls or worn-looking blue jeans—a man no longer even middle-aged, bent over a hoe, turning the soil over; his wife in her plaid shirt, hoeing along-side him.

I think my mother must have had that book memo-rized, she read it so often. All those two had was each other, she said. That was enough.

Maybe there was some guilt involved—the feeling that my mother needed me, and my father didn't—that brought me to my decision, but the truth is, I think I needed my mother. I missed our conversations over dinner, and the way—unlike Marjorie, who seemed to use a whole other vocal register when talking with anybody under twenty-one years old—she never spoke with me any differently than she would to a person her own age. Though with a few exceptions—the occasional door-to-door solicitor, her MegaMite customers, and the oil-delivery man—the only person she spoke with was me.

By the following spring, when I told my father I wanted to go back and live at my mother's house, he didn't argue. The next day, I moved back into our old place.

I tried out for the baseball team. They put me in right field. One time, when we were playing the team Richard was on, I caught a long fly ball he hit, that everyone expected to be a triple. Every time I came up to bat, I had this ritual. *See the ball,* I said, too softly for even the catcher to hear. More often than you might think, I got a hit.

My mother and I lived, all my high school years, in a house without possessions, more or less. We had a few items of furniture left from that day we thought we were leaving forever, but except for the things we'd put in boxes in the car, we'd given away just about everything, and even of what we'd kept, intending to take it with us for our new life up north, we hardly took anything out of the boxes, besides the coffeemaker and a few items of clothing. Not my mother's wardrobe of dancing outfits, or her amazing shoes and scarves, her fans, or the paintings that used to hang on our walls, or her dulcimer, or her tape player even, though eventually, when I started earning my own money, I bought a Walkman, so I could listen to my music.

The voices of Frank Sinatra and Joni Mitchell and (now I knew his name) Leonard Cohen were no longer heard in our house. No more *Guys and Dolls* sound track. Or any music. No music, no dancing.

At some point, after it was over, we made a trip to the Goodwill, where my mother bought back just enough plates and forks and cups for the two of us to have our meals, though when you eat frozen dinners and soup most of the time, you don't need much in the way of dishes. In tenth grade, though, I took a home economics class—they had started opening these kinds of courses up to boys by this point. I discovered I liked to cook, and for some reason, though my mother knew virtually nothing about cooking, I was good at it. One of my specialties, not learned in home economics, was pie.

For most of high school, my father and I continued our tradition of going out to dinner Saturday nights, though when my social life picked up, as it did eventually, we switched to weeknights, and to everyone's relief, probably, Marjorie stopped accompanying us.

I got along well enough with Richard, and I got to enjoy hanging out with my little sister, Chloe, on occasion, but restaurant nights were mostly just my father and me, and at my suggestion, we changed the venue from Friendly's to a place a little outside of town called Acropolis that served Greek food, which was better, and once, when Marjorie was out of town visiting her sister, I even went over to their house and made a dish I'd seen in a magazine, chicken marsala.

One night, over spanakopita at Acropolis—under the influence of a couple of glasses of red wine—my father tackled the topic of sex, that had remained dormant, more or less, since his first early attempts to fill me in on the facts of life.

Everybody talks about all this crazy, wild passion, he said. That's how it goes, in the songs. Your mother was like that. She was in love with love. She couldn't do anything partway. She felt everything so deeply, it was like the world was too much for her. Any time she'd hear a story about some kid who had cancer, or an old man whose wife died, or his dog even, it was like it happened to her. It was like she was missing the outer layer of skin that allows people to get through the day without bleeding all the time. The world got to be too much for her.

Me, I'd just as soon stay a little bit numb, he said. Whatever it is I'm missing, that's OK by me.

I was going home from the library one day—a place I hung out often, during the months I lived with my father and Marjorie. It was a holiday weekend—Columbus Day maybe, or more likely, Veterans Day. I remember the leaves were off the trees by this point, and it got dark early, so that by the time I'd return to the house for dinner, the lights would be on throughout the neighborhood. Riding my bike home—or, as I was that night, walking—I could look in the windows and see the people who lived inside, doing all the things people do in their houses. It was like moving through a museum with a whole row of brightly lit dioramas, labeled something like *How People Live* or *Families in America.* A woman chopping up vegetables at the sink. A man reading the newspaper. A couple of kids in an upstairs bedroom, playing Twister. A girl lying on her bed, talking on the phone.

There was an apartment building on this street—an old house that had been turned into condominiums, probably—where I always looked up. There was this one particular apartment whose windows I liked studying, where the family always seemed to be sitting down to dinner at just about the same hour every day, which happened to be when I was passing this particular corner. It was sort of a superstition with me, you might say, that if I saw the three of them—the father, the mother, and the little boy—gathered around the table, as I generally did, nothing terrible was going to happen that night. I think the person I was worried about not getting through the night, at that point, was my mother. Who would be sitting at her table alone right about then. Having her glass of wine, reading her *Good Life* book.

This family just always looked so happy and homey was the thing. More than any of the other family dioramas in the *How People Live* museum, I wished this was the one I was coming home to. You couldn't hear what the people were saying, naturally, but you didn't have to, to know things were going well in that kitchen. The conversation probably wasn't especially earth-shattering (*How was your day, honey? Fine, how about yours?*) but something about the feeling around that table—the soft yellow light, the nodding faces, the way the woman touched the man's arm, and how they laughed when the little boy waved his spoon around— gave you the impression there was no place else they'd rather be at that moment, or anyone they'd rather be with than each other.

I guess maybe I'd forgotten where I was, and I was just standing there. It was a cold night—cold enough that I could see my breath, and see the breath of the person coming down the steps of the apartment building, with a little dog on a leash, so little she might have been walking a feather duster. Smaller than the smallest poodle, even.

Even before I recognized her face, I understood I knew the person walking the dog, I just didn't know from where. All I could see was skinny legs under an oversize black coat, and high-heeled boots, which people didn't usually wear in our town. Never, actually.

It was plain that she hadn't taken this dog on very many walks before tonight, or if she had, she had an unusually stupid dog on her hands. Because he kept on getting tangled up, twisting his leash around her legs and jumping up and going from one side to the other— pulling tight on the leash one second, releasing altogether and sitting motionless a moment later.

Heel, Jim, the voice said.

This had about as much effect as if I'd told my mother, *You should get out more. Make new friends. Take a trip.* When the voice said this, the little dog went crazier than ever. He must have bitten her leg or something, because she let go of the leash, or lost control completely anyway, so now the dog was tearing down the sidewalk—*Jim? Who names their dog Jim?*—and straight for the corner, where a truck was barreling down.

I dove to catch him. Somehow, I did. The person with the skinny legs came running up to me then, dragging a very large purse and wobbling in the high-heeled boots. She had been wearing a hat—a wide-brimmed hat, with a feather or something sprouting out the top, and that had fallen off, which made it easier to see her face. This was when I realized it was Eleanor. Now here she was, tottering down the street, straight in my direction.

In those first weeks after that Labor Day, when the world was simply spinning, I couldn't think clearly about anything. When I felt anger—and I did—it was all directed at myself. That never went away, but after a while, I recognized another object for my anger, and that was Eleanor.

It was the first time I'd seen her since that day we'd met for coffee when she'd jumped on top of me. She had not enrolled in my school that fall, and since nobody knew her, there was nobody to ask about her, even if I'd wanted to. I figured she'd gone back to Chicago, to stir up trouble there. She would have found someone to have sex with by this point, probably. It was so clear, from our brief acquaintance, that not remaining a virgin for even ten more minutes was one of her goals.

She might have ignored me—bent to pick up her hat and kept on walking—except that I had her dog. He was pressed up against my chest, and even through the fabric of my jacket I could feel his heart beating fast, the way it used to be with Joe the hamster back when he was around.

That's my dog, she said, reaching out for him, like a shopper waiting for her change.

I'm holding him hostage, I said. Normally, I would never have made a remark like that. It just came out.

What are you talking about? she said. He's mine.

You told the police about Frank, I said. Until now, I had never acknowledged this, even to myself, but suddenly I knew.

You basically ruined two people's lives, I said.

I want my dog, she said.

Oh yeah, I told her. Now that I was started, I was in the zone. I might have been channeling Magnum P.I. or someone. What's it worth to you? I asked her.

If you must know, Jim is a purebred shih tzu. He cost four hundred and twenty-five dollars, not counting the shots. But that's not the point. He belongs to me. Give him back.

Up until this moment, when I'd thought about what Eleanor had done, the part I focused on was how mad she'd been at me, for not making mad passionate love to her by the swings that day she took her underpants off. I was enough of a dope, I hadn't even paid much attention to the part about the reward. Now—a year after it happened, probably, maybe two—hearing her mention her four-hundred-and-twenty-five-dollar puppy, that I'd just rescued from getting run over, it came to me.

I guess a person that got ten thousand dollars for ratting out someone's mother can spare a few hundred for a furball, I said.

My father gave him to me, she said. He's taking care of Jim while I'm away at school.

So you got to go to your fancy arts academy after all, I said. I still had my hand around the little dog's belly. It had sunk in now, where his name came from. Maybe the dog was trying to do himself in, along the lines of his namesake, I said. When heroin's unavailable, getting squashed by a truck might have to suffice.

You are so sick, she said. No wonder you don't have any friends.

I don't suppose you care, I told her. But the man the police took away that day was probably the best person I know.

I made this statement for effect, but after I said it, I realized that this was actually true. Just hearing the words, I did something I hated. I started to cry.

This was definitely the moment for her to come back at me with her old standby—that I was a loser. There wasn't any doubt now, she was getting her dog back. I wasn't what you could call an intimidating person at that point.

She didn't move. She just stood there in her high heels, holding her ridiculous hat and her oversize purse that looked like something she'd taken from the dress-up box. She may have been even thinner than ever—it was hard to tell, with her coat on. There were dark circles under her eyes, and her mouth had a pinched quality. I no longer believed she could have had sex with anybody. She looked like someone who, if you touched her, might snap.

I didn't know, she said. I just wanted something to happen. She was crying too.

Well, it did, all right, I told her. I handed her the dog. Although I had only been holding him about a minute, he had started licking my hand. I got the feeling he might have preferred staying with me. Even a dog would know—maybe a dog, most of all—that Eleanor wasn't the type of person you'd want to hang around more than absolutely necessary.

I saw her again a few years later, at a party given by a guy at my school, who was in the drama crowd. She had a little silver amulet type of thing that she wore around her neck, with cocaine in it, and she was putting some on a mirror and snorting it, and some other people were doing that too, but I didn't. She was still thin, but not like before. She had those same eyes, with the whites showing all around. She pretended not to know me but I knew she remembered, though I had nothing to say to her anymore. I'd said enough—way too much—already.

I finally went to bed with a girl in junior year. I probably could have done it sooner. The opportunity came up, as it had with Eleanor, but I had this idea that seemed a little old-fashioned at the time, that I shouldn't do it with a girl unless I loved her, and I wanted her to love me too, which Becky did. We were together right through graduation, and the first half of freshman year at college, until she met some boy she was crazy about, and evidently she married him. I thought for a while I'd never get over her, but I did, of course. You think many things will be true, when you're nineteen years old.

My mother continued to sell MegaMite over the phone, now and then, from our kitchen table, and she believed forever that it was my own regular dose of the stuff that had been responsible for my attaining the height of six foot one, though neither of my parents could have been called a tall person.

You are the tallest person I know, my mother told me once.

No, actually, she said. That isn't true. We both knew who she was thinking about then, though nobody said his name.

Sometime after I left home, my mother got what Marjorie might have termed a real job. Not that it paid any better than selling vitamins had, but it got her out of our house, finally. Maybe it was my leaving that made her know that she needed to get out more.

She took herself down to the senior center in our town. She offered her services, teaching dancing. Foxtrot, waltz, two-step, swing—all the old partner dances, though given the ratio of women to men at that place, a lot of the women had to take the man's part when she taught. She turned out to be a great teacher, and another good thing about the senior center was that you hardly ever saw any babies there.

She was so popular with her students that pretty soon they had her running their entire activities program at the center. This included crafts projects and game nights, and sometimes she'd set up a totally wacky scavenger hunt that the geezers could do even in wheelchairs. Working with the old-timers that way seemed to make my mother younger again. Seeing her with them, sometimes, when she was demonstrating a waltz turn or a fancy move in the Lindy—trim as ever; she never lost her figure—I could see a faint trace of the look I remembered from that handful of days back when I was thirteen. The long Labor Day weekend that Frank Chambers came to stay.

Chapter 22

Eighteen years passed. I was thirty-one years old—losing my hair, or starting to—living in up-state New York. Living, then as now, with my girl-friend, Amelia, the woman I would marry that fall. We had a little rented house overlooking the Hudson—uninsulated, so sometimes, when the wind came up off the river in winter, the only way to stay warm was to light a fire and sit there with a blanket over us, holding on to each other. Nothing wrong with that, Amelia said. If you don't want to rub up against a person, why would you want to be with them in the first place?

It was a lucky life. Amelia taught kindergarten and played the banjo in a little bluegrass band that also included—surprisingly—my stepbrother, Richard, on stand-up bass. I'd finished culinary school four years earlier. I had a job as a pastry chef in a small town nearby, in a restaurant that had recently started getting a surprising amount of attention. That summer we'd be heading to New Hampshire for the wedding—just our families and a dozen friends.

The summer before, a writer from New York City, on the staff of a glossy food magazine of the sort that only people who hardly ever have time to cook can afford, had paid a visit to the restaurant. This magazine seemed to specialize in articles about parties people held in their apple orchard or on an island in Maine, or on the shore of some lake in Montana, where the hosts caught their own fish but somehow, miraculously, had ten friends nearby who were all tall, good-looking, and totally cool, to come over and share it with them on a harvest table set up along the banks of the trout stream where the fish had been caught.

The idea was to show beautiful pictures of amazing foods people grew on organic farms, or dishes some great-grandmother nobody ever really had might have prepared in an old wood-fired oven, though the people they tended to feature in their photographs didn't resemble anybody's relatives that I knew, or live the kind of lives people who grew this produce and created these dishes in the first place actually had.

This particular writer had heard about the restaurant where I was dessert chef, and paid a visit. The recipe she decided on, to feature in the magazine—a full-page photograph—had been my raspberry-peach pie.

Some things about this pie were my invention. The use of crystallized ginger in the filling for instance. The addition of fresh raspberries. But the crust was Frank's. Or, as I explained it in the article, Frank's grandmother's. So was the choice, for a thickener, of Minute tapioca, over cornstarch.

I didn't explain, in the pages of *Nouveau Gourmet,* the exact circumstances under which I'd learned my piecrust technique. I said only that a friend had taught me, and that he had learned at the elbow of his grandmother, on the Christmas-tree farm where he'd grown up. I said I was thirteen years old when I first learned to make pie, and I mentioned in the article the particular serendipity of having been presented with a bucket of fresh peaches that day, and the challenge of preparing piecrust in the middle of a heat wave.

It's important to keep your ingredients chilled, I said.

It's easier adding water than taking it out. Never overhandle the dough.

Never mind all that expensive equipment they sell in catalogs, I said. The heel of your hand is the perfect tool for patching crust.

About placing the top crust over the fruit: here was the one act in the process where the baker must simply plunge into the unknown. The one thing you must never do here: hesitate. Flipping that crust over is a leap of faith, I said. Like jumping out a window—twelve hours after undergoing an emergency appendectomy, perhaps—and believing, as you leapt, that you would land on your two feet.

After that article came out, I was invited to appear on a local morning television program in Syracuse, as Chef of the Week, to demonstrate my piecrust technique. I got a surprising number of letters from readers of the magazine, and then viewers of the television program, asking for advice about their own piecrust issues. It seemed everybody had some. I don't know another food that seems to inspire stronger emotion—passion, even—than that most humble of desserts, pie.

As Frank had warned me once, the topic of shortening inspired the greatest controversy. One woman who'd read in the magazine that I used a combination of lard and butter for my shortening wrote to tell me all about the evils of lard. Another woman took equally strong exception to my use of butter.

Meanwhile, the restaurant, Molly's Table, was doing better than ever. Amelia and I put money down on a house, and I put up storm windows. The owner of the restaurant—Molly—hired me to run a specialty pie shop next door, where I supervised a staff of five bakers, all making pies to the specifications passed on to me from Frank.

Almost a full year after the article ran in the magazine, I received a letter with an unfamiliar postmark, from someplace in Idaho. The envelope was addressed in pencil, and the return address featured not a name, but a long series of numbers.

Inside, on lined notebook paper, in very neat and precise handwriting, but very small—as if the author of the letter had been conserving paper, which he probably had, by necessity—was a letter.

I sat down then. Until this moment, I hadn't understood, but now it came back to me, like a blast of cold air when you open the door in a snowstorm, or the heat from a five-hundred-degree oven when you open it to check on—what else?—the pie. It all came back to me.

Though nearly two decades had passed, I could still see his face as it had been the day I met him in the magazine section at Pricemart—the bones of his jaw, those hollow cheeks, the way he looked me square in the eye, with those blue eyes of his. Young as I was, small as I was—a boy who longed to discover what might lie within the sealed packaging of the September 1987 issue of *Playboy*, who had to settle for a puzzle book instead—he might have seemed like an intimidating person. I could see him now, looming over me as he did that day—such a tall man, with those big hands and that impossibly deep voice. But I had felt, the moment I first met him, that I could trust this person, and even when I was angriest and most fearful— that he might take my mother away, that I'd be left alone, displaced—that sense of him as a fair and decent man had never left me.

I'd heard nothing of the man in nearly twenty years, and I got a feeling, as I unfolded the piece of paper from inside the envelope—a single sheet, nothing more—identical to the one I had all those years ago, riding in my mother's car back to our house with him in the backseat. That feeling that life was about to change. The world would be different soon. This had been good news, the first time. Now what I registered was dread.

Sitting at the counter of the restaurant kitchen, surrounded by my bowls and knives, my Viking stove, my oak cutting block, I heard his low voice speaking to me.

Dear Henry,

I hope you will remember me. Though perhaps it would have been better for us all if you'd forgotten. We spent Labor Day weekend together, many years ago. Six of the best days of my life.

Sometimes, he wrote, people donated boxes of old magazines to the library at the prison where he was currently incarcerated. This was how he had come to see the article in the magazine, concerning my pies. First off, he wanted to congratulate me on my accomplishment, at having graduated from culinary school. He'd always liked to cook himself, though as I had evidently remembered, baking had been his specialty too. And in fact, if I ever wanted to hear about biscuit making, he had some thoughts on that.

Meanwhile, he was proud and happy to read that a skill he had passed on so long ago had stayed with me.

As you get older, it's nice to think you might have contributed some small piece of wisdom or know-how to someone, somewhere along the line. But in a case like mine, with no children of my own to raise, and having spent most of my adult life in a correctional institution, the opportunities to impart knowledge of any kind to a young person have been limited. Though I do also recall a few interesting sessions in which you and I played catch, where you displayed more talent than you had previously imagined.

He was writing now, he told me, with a question. He did not wish to disrupt my life or that of my family—ever again—or cause additional disturbance, as surely our brief acquaintance with him, so long ago, must have done. The reason he was writing this to me, and not to the individual his question most directly concerned, in fact, had to do with his extreme concern about ever again causing pain to the one person, more than any other on this planet, to whom he would least wish to bring sorrow.

I will understand if you choose not to respond to this letter. Your silence would be as much word as I would need, to discontinue any thought of further communication.

He would be released on parole shortly. He had of course had plenty of time to think about what he would do after leaving prison the following month. Although he was no longer even close to young—he'd recently marked his fifty-eighth birthday—he was still in good health, with plenty of energy left for hard work. It was his hope that he might find work as a handyman some- where, or perhaps a housepainter, or—this was his first choice—that he might work on a farm again, as he had when he was a boy. Besides his time with us, those were his fondest memories.

But one thought haunted him, he said. It might ac- tually be a relief, if I wrote to tell him this was foolish and crazy, but he had never gotten my mother out of his mind. Very likely she was remarried now, and living with a husband somewhere, far away from the town where we'd met. If so—if she was happy and well—it would make him happy to know that. He would never bother her, or intrude in any way in the life she had made for herself. My mother was a woman long overdue for happiness, he wrote.

> But on the chance that she might be alone, I wanted to ask you whether you thought I might write her a letter. I promise you, I would sooner cut off my own hand than bring grief to Adele.

He wrote down his address for me then, along with the date of his release. He signed the letter *Truly Yours. Frank Chambers.*

Here was a man who had trusted me, when I was thirteen years old, not to betray him, and I had. My actions over the course of that handful of days had robbed him of a life—eighteen years of it—he might have known with my mother, a woman who loved him.

I had betrayed my mother too, of course. Those five nights she and Frank spent together represented the only time, in more than twenty years, that she'd shared her bed with any man. I had thought, at the time, that nothing could be worse than to lie in the dark, listening to the sounds of the two of them making love, but later I learned: worse was the silence on the other side of the wall.

In his letter, Frank made no mention of my role in what had taken place the day the police cars came for him. Or of my mother's willingness to let the authorities believe he had tied us up and held us against our will. He spoke only of one thing: his wish to see her again, if she were willing.

I wrote him back that day to say that it would not be difficult to locate my mother, and less difficult to locate his place in her heart. She still lived at our same address.

Chapter 23

S ex is a drug, Eleanor had told me. When sex enters into a situation, people lose all reason. They do things they would never do otherwise. These things they do may be crazy. May even be dangerous. May break their hearts, or someone else's.

To Eleanor, and to my own thirteen-year-old self, maybe—lying on my narrow single bed, pressed up against the wall on whose other side was my mother's bed, with her in it, making love to Frank—the story of what happened in our family that long hot weekend was only about sex. To my thirteen-year-old self that summer, everything was about sex, in one way or another, though in the end, when the opportunity had been presented to me, to discover it—*try the drug*—I chose not to.

The real drug, I came to believe, was love. Rare love, for which no explanation might be found. A man dropped out of a second-story window and ran, bleeding, into a discount department store. A woman drove him home. They were two people who could not go out into the world, who made a world with each other, inside the too-thin walls of our old yellow house. For a little less than six days they held on to each other for dear life. For nineteen years, he had waited for the moment when he could return to her. Finally, he did.

Because of his status as a convicted felon, emigration to Canada was not possible, so they moved as close to the border as they could, to Maine. It's a long drive from upstate New York, and a little difficult, with a baby. Still, we go there more often than you might think.

When our daughter cries, we pull the car over by the side of the road and unbuckle her seat belt, and just hold her. Sometimes the place we pull over may be inconvenient for this. An interstate highway, more than likely. Or we might be only twenty minutes from their house—close enough that you might say, never mind, push on through.

But I always stop to hold our daughter. Or one of us does. If there are large trucks barreling past, we may walk down the embankment, away from the noise a little. Or I'll cup my hands over her ears. If there's grass, I may lie down in it, and lay her on the bare skin of my chest—or if it's winter, buckle her inside my jacket, or place a handful of snow on her tongue, and if it's night, we may look at the stars for a minute. What I have found is that a baby—though she doesn't know words yet, or information, or the rules of life—is the most reliable judge of feelings. All a baby has with which to take in the world are her five senses. Hold her, sing to her, show her the night sky or a quivering leaf, or a bug. Those are the ways—the only ways—she learns about the world—whether it is a safe and loving place, or a harsh one.

What she will register, at least, will be the fact that she is not alone. And it has been my experience that when you do this—slow down, pay attention, follow the simple instincts of love—a person is likely to respond favorably. It is generally true of babies, and most other people too, perhaps. Also dogs. Hamsters even. And people so damaged by life in the world that there might seem no hope for them, only there may be.

So I talk to her. Sometimes we dance. When our daughter's breathing is steady again—maybe she has fallen asleep, maybe not—we buckle her up in her car seat and continue north. I always know, whatever hour it may be when we pull down the long dirt road leading to their house, that the lights will be on, and the door will be open even before we reach it—my mother standing there, with Frank beside her.

You brought the baby, she says.

HARPER LUXE

THE NEW LUXURY IN READING

We hope you enjoyed reading
our new, comfortable print size and found it
an experience you would like to repeat.

Well – you're in luck!

HarperLuxe offers the finest in fiction and
nonfiction books in this same larger print size and
paperback format. Light and easy to read, HarperLuxe
paperbacks are for book lovers who want to see
what they are reading without the strain.

For a full listing of titles and
new releases to come, please visit our website:

www.HarperLuxe.com